BEFORE HER LAST BREATH

A SAM LAWSON MYSTERY
BOOK 6

DAVID K. WILSON

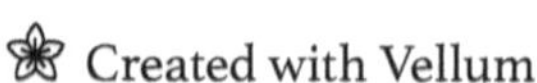 Created with Vellum

1

———

Wednesday, 6:45 p.m.

By the time she saw him, it was too late.

She tried to fight back against the hulking man, but his massive arms wrapped tightly around her, pinning her back against his chest.

Then, as she struggled to break free, she caught his reflection in a mirror.

It was the face of a dead man.

He had been killed in a shootout just a few hours earlier. Or at least that's what she had been told. That's why she had let down her guard. Why she had come home without a police escort. She had been preparing to take a shower and had stripped down to her underwear when he came out of nowhere and grabbed her from behind.

She stared at his face to be sure. It was definitely him. She saw the menacing glare in his eyes. The sneering lip. Then she noticed the hypodermic needle in his free hand. She knew he had subdued his previous victims with a barely-less-than-lethal dose of ketamine before dragging them away.

She began to fight back with all her strength. She tried kicking him. Elbowing him. Anything to throw him off his game. But he was too strong. A jolt of panic shot through her as she felt the sting of the needle pierce her neck.

Maybe her fiancé would get home in time. Maybe he could stop this. Then another thought hit her. If he arrived too late, how would he know she was abducted? There was no real sign of a struggle. He'd have no reason to suspect foul play. He'd just think she had gone out with friends. By the time he realized something was wrong, it could be too late.

As she felt her body grow limp and numb, she knew she only had seconds. She wildly flailed her arms, using her thumb to discreetly push her engagement ring off her finger. In the corner of her eye, she saw it roll to the corner of the bedroom.

And then everything went black.

2

7:15 p.m.

HE BOLTED INTO THE HOUSE, yelling her name. He'd been phoning her non-stop for the past half-hour, but the calls had been going straight to voice mail. It wasn't like her to turn her phone off. As the Hubbard County Medical Examiner, she was on call 24/7 and always had her phone by her side.

The house looked normal. No signs of struggles or forced entry anywhere. He saw her work clothes laid out on the edge of the bed, so he knew she had come home after work. It all seemed perfectly normal. But then why was his gut twisted into a knot?

Why was this happening? Why her?

. . .

Sam Lawson and his fiancé Carla Davenport had taken every precaution since receiving the first threatening note from Ken Mullen, a serial killer who, just a few months earlier, Sam knew only as an old friend and ex-partner. Then Sam discovered his old friend was the infamous Replacement Killer, a ruthless murderer responsible for dozens and dozens of deaths over the past few decades. He received his moniker because of he typically wouldn't kill a victim until he had abducted a new one. Unfortunately, before Sam could make an arrest, Mullen had escaped.

Not long after, the couple had received a threatening note from Mullen with a veiled threat toward Carla. Sam had immediately beefed up their home security and Carla even had a police officer escort her home every day. But then Sam had supposedly killed Mullen in a shoot-out. Mullen had fallen off a cliff into the rushing rapids below. Sam had called Carla to tell her the FBI was confident the river had washed Mullen's body downstream into the alligator-infested river bottom. But she didn't know what Sam discovered after that call: That Mullen had faked his death. He had pretended to fall off the cliff, hiding on a hidden ledge and sneaking away before Sam could see him.

FBI Agent Terry Goldsmith had assumed Mullen had faked his death to stop any manhunt for him. But now Carla was missing.

It made no sense. Why would Mullen go to all of that trouble to disappear just so he could reemerge to take Carla? That would put the radar right back on him.

Sam sat on the edge of the bed and tried calling Carla one more time. Her voice mail picked up almost immediately. He groaned and tried to calm himself down, trying to come up with a different theory than an abduction.

He had almost started to buy his own pep talk when he noticed something odd on her vanity. Her jewelry case was open. For most people that would mean nothing, but Carla was fastidious about her jewelry. She had a place for every earring and necklace and always carefully shut the case's lid.

Sam examined the case. Everything seemed in place. Nothing out of the ordinary. Then he noticed there was only one blue gemstone earring. He looked through the case for the other one but found nothing. Then he looked around the table and the floor. Sam knew Carla well enough to know she would have noticed the missing earring, too. And she would have scoured the room until she found it.

A sparkle in the corner of the room, near the bathroom door, caught Sam's attention. He walked toward it and his heart did a free-fall.

It was Carla's engagement ring.

Unless she was examining a corpse, Carla never

took her ring off. Ever. And even if she did, why would it be lying in a corner on the floor? He knew there was only one explanation. As he stared at the ring on the floor, he dialed a number into his phone again.

"Ramirez? He was here. And he's got Carla."

3

____

7:20 p.m.

Wilton Police Detective Joe Ramirez, along with a team of uniformed officers and forensic experts, descended upon the house within minutes.

Sam explained what he had discovered to Ramirez, who normally would have been skeptical. But as soon as Sam had called, Ramirez sent an officer down to the morgue in search for Carla and sent two squad cars to patrol the town's limited choice in restaurants. Carla was nowhere to be seen. And the fact that her phone went straight to voicemail was more convincing than a runaway engagement ring.

"How long have you been home?" he asked Sam.

"Not long," Sam answered. "Fifteen minutes tops."

Ramirez got Carla's car information from Sam and called in an APB.

Sam was beginning to panic.

"Why was she home alone?" he yelled. "Where were your guys?"

"Sam, she's the one who called off the police escort," Ramirez said. "We all thought he was dead."

"What do we know?" a voice asked.

It was FBI agent Terry Goldsmith, the agent who had been heading up the search for the Replacement Killer long before he was identified as Ken Mullen.

Ramirez repeated everything that Sam had told him while Sam watched a team of federal agents take over his home, setting up different boxes of electronic equipment on his dining table and kitchen island.

Goldsmith put a hand on Sam's shoulder.

"We'll get her back," he said.

"We don't even know where she is," Sam muttered. He pointed to the equipment being set up. "And is that necessary?"

"It's for phone tracking and recording," Goldsmith answered.

Sam shook his head.

"I know what it's for," Sam said. "But Mullen isn't going to call for ransom."

"It's standard operating procedure," Goldsmith said.

"And we have to be ready for anything. He's already broken from his normal pattern once."

"I hate to be the one to say it," Ramirez interrupted. "But we don't even know if Mullen did this."

Sam shot him a glare that let him know there was no doubt in his mind. And, truth be told, Ramirez didn't have much doubt himself.

"We're blocking off all roads," Goldsmith said. "And we still have the chopper we were already using for Mullen's manhunt. We'll find her."

4

───────

Thursday, 3:00 a.m.

As HIS OLD brown and white Ford truck drove down the lonely state highway, Ken Mullen whistled a happy, carefree tune. He grabbed the silver canister in his cupholder and stopped whistling just long enough to take a sip of the now-lukewarm coffee. He glanced at his watch and then at his phone that was nestled in one of the car's cup holders. It was 3:00 a.m. The ketamine tranquilizer he had given Carla would wear off soon. The timing couldn't be any better.

He slowed down as he neared a metal gate on the side of the highway. It was so unassuming that any other car would have driven right past it without noticing.

Mullen pulled in front of the gate and got out of the truck. He pulled a key from his pocket and, with the help of the truck's headlights, found the padlock that secured the gate. With a twist of the key, he opened the lock, pulled the chain through the two gate panels, and pushed them open. After driving through the gate, he stopped to lock it behind him. While it was highly unlikely anyone would have followed him, years of working on both sides of the law had taught him to never leave anything to chance.

As Mullen walked back to the truck, he pounded on the fiberglass topper mounted over the rear bed.

"Wakey wakey, eggs and bakey!"

Mullen drove slowly down the bumpy dirt road. He felt confident he was alone, but cut the headlights just the same. Driving in the dark on the winding road was treacherous, and he was only able to navigate it because he knew the path so well.

Finally, he arrived at a small cabin in the middle of nowhere. After gulping down the last bit of coffee, he cut the engine, stepped out of the truck, and started whistling again.

He looked up to take in the starry night sky. With no city lights or streetlights, the sky was blanketed in a swath of sparkling stars. He could make out the Milky Way, as well as all the familiar constellations. He grinned as he caught the streaking light from a falling star.

"Make a wish," he muttered to himself.

He grabbed a small canvas case from behind his seat and walked to the back of the truck. He lifted the truck topper's rear window, switched on the service light and looked inside. Mullen had covered the topper's side windows with black tape. A twin-size mattress lay in the middle of the truck bed with bags of feed on either side to keep it from sliding. Lying in the middle of the mattress was an unconscious Carla Davenport.

Mullen admired her lean body as he climbed into the truck bed. He knelt beside her and pushed a strand of brown hair off her face so he could see her better. How Sam wound up with such a good-looking woman was beyond him. He stared at her exposed body and lost himself in a moment of desire. But he quickly shook the thoughts out of his mind.

"I'll get a shirt for you when we get inside," he whispered.

He checked to make sure the plastic cable tie that bound her wrists together was still strong, then checked the other tie that secured her ankles. Satisfied everything was still intact, he turned her over to grab a roll of duct tape that had slid under her legs.

Carla began to stir, and Mullen's smile widened.

"There's my Sleeping Beauty."

He watched as Carla slowly came to, excitedly looking forward to the moment when she realized her predicament. Carla moaned quietly. Her eyelids opened, and she blinked as she tried to pull herself out of her drug-induced sleep. When she realized her arms and legs were bound, she began to panic. Then she looked up to see Mullen smiling down at her. Before she could even open her mouth to protest, he slapped a piece of duct tape over it, muffling her voice.

"Save your energy, Carla," he said. "You're going to need it."

The panic in her eyes quickly shifted to anger and, even though she was still groggy from the drugs, she mumbled a string of muffled words. While he wasn't able to understand what she was saying, he had a pretty good idea, and he shook his head in disapproval.

"Sticks and stones, Carla. Sticks and stones."

He grabbed the small canvas case. As Carla writhed, he unzipped it and removed a syringe and needle. Her eyes widened, and she attempted to lift her body to escape, but she was still too weak. Mullen shushed her as he pulled out a small vile and injected the needle into it.

"Don't worry," he said gently. "You'll be back to sleep before you know it."

He smiled as he tapped the syringe.

"Hold still," he said, gripping Carla's shoulder to steady her. "This is gonna sting a little."

He pinned her arm down with his knee and injected her with the sedative. As soon as he let go of her, she began to wriggle and fight.

"Be careful. You're gonna hurt yourself," he taunted, leaning down close to her face. "And that's my job."

He climbed out of the truck and pulled Carla out toward him. She wriggled and fought as hard as she could, but the little strength she had was fading fast.

"Damn, woman. You're like a big fish," he laughed. "Be still or I might drop you."

He held her legs down and waited. Within a minute, the sedative took effect, and Carla's body went limp again. Mullen lifted Carla out with little more than a grunt, throwing her over his shoulder and carrying her inside.

5

4:30 a.m.

SAM PACED THE ROOM NERVOUSLY, as he had been doing all night. Most of the other officers and federal agents, including Goldsmith, were scattered on the couch and living room chairs "resting their eyes". Only Ramirez stayed awake with Sam.

"We need to be out there. Doing something!" Sam said.

"We've got local, county and federal officers blocking roads, checking leads and going through traffic surveillance videos," Ramirez said. "The best thing you can do is wait here."

"For what? He's not calling for a ransom."

Ramirez rubbed his eyes, as much from being tired as from being tired of this conversation. "You know we can't make any assumptions."

Before Sam could argue back, the phone rang. It startled everyone awake, and they immediately jumped into action. Sam instinctively reached for his cellphone then realized it wasn't what was ringing. All eyes turned to the source.

"It's the landline," Sam said.

Goldsmith looked at the FBI technicians to see if they were up and ready. When they nodded, he directed Sam to the phone.

Sam checked again to make sure everyone was ready and then answered.

"Hello?"

"Hey, Sam. Miss me?"

Sam immediately recognized Mullen's voice. His pulse raced, and he nodded at Goldsmith, who started silently directing the technicians to track the call.

"If you so much as harm a hair on her head, I swear to God I'll kill you," Sam said.

"Relax. She's fine. For now."

Goldsmith mouthed the words "Tone it down" to Sam. Sam shot the FBI agent the finger.

"Where are you?" Sam asked.

"Oh, let me send you the coordinates," Mullen replied with a laugh. "It's not that easy, Sam. And I know your FBI buddies are listening in. Hi, boys. Don't bother tracking the call. I'm ghosting the signal."

"You're not as smart as you think you are," Sam said. "I'm gonna find you. And you're going to pay for this."

"I've got a deal for you, Sammy. How about a trade? You for her."

"Where and when, asshole?"

"Shhhh. That's a secret. For your ears only. Get in that precious truck of yours and start driving west on 16. Alone. And I've got video monitors along the way. I'll know. Once I know you're free of the feds, I'll call you."

Sam looked at the FBI techs. They shook their heads. Mullen has been telling the truth. He had somehow ghosted his call, and they weren't able to track it. Still, Sam tried to prolong the conversation.

"How long do I need to drive?"

"Until I call you. And I need you to drive the speed limit. No speeding. But don't go any slower, either. And Sam, I know you're not good at following orders, but if you mess this up, if I so much as suspect someone is following you or you deviate from my orders, I'll happily make your pretty little fiancé my next victim."

And then he hung up.

"I've got to go," Sam said immediately.

"You're not going anywhere by yourself," Goldsmith said.

"You heard him," Sam argued. "He said come alone.

And he's an ex-cop. He'll spot a tail from a mile away. I won't risk that."

"Sam, come on," Ramirez said. "It's clearly a trap."

"Of course it's a trap," Sam snapped. "But it's Carla's best chance. Look. I'll call in as I go so you can keep tabs on my location."

"Absolutely not," Ramirez said. "He'll just kill you both. You're not thinking straight."

Sam nodded and tried to calm himself down.

"No. You need to do it," Goldsmith interjected.

Sam and Ramirez both turned to the FBI agent.

"You go alone. And call in your location as you go, like you said," Goldsmith said. "We'll tag team behind you off of different vehicles, so it doesn't look like a tail."

Sam started to argue, but Goldsmith stopped him.

"Chances are, he's not going to give you his location all at once. He'll piece it to you. Probably use landmarks along the way. At some point, I'm guessing it will get remote enough that any car following you would be obvious. We won't follow any further, but we'll listen. We can put a tracking device on your truck. And on you. He's probably going to have you go on foot at some point. Once we see you've stopped, we're coming in."

"You can't let him go out there alone," Ramirez argued.

"We need to get this guy," Goldsmith replied. "These

are the cards we've been dealt, so we're gonna play them."

Sam nodded.

"Let's get going."

6

5:00 a.m.

IT TOOK LESS than five minutes for the FBI to plant a tracker on Sam's truck and another under the collar of his blue denim shirt. Sam climbed into the truck, but before shutting the door, he turned to Goldsmith and Ramirez.

"If you're tailing me too close, I will lose you," he warned.

"You won't even know we're there," Goldsmith assured him. "And if you have any concerns, just say them out loud. We put a mic in the truck so we can listen to everything."

"And I can hear you?" Sam asked.

"Unfortunately, no," Goldsmith said. "We weren't

fully prepared for this and only had a one-way transmitter. Sorry."

Sam smirked. "You just want to talk behind my back."

He shut the truck door and backed out of his long gravel driveway. Goldsmith immediately motioned at two agents sitting in an older model gold Chrysler Imperial.

"Give him five minutes, then head out," he said as he walked over to a light blue van with a large "Dan's Plumbing" logo painted on the side.

"You come with me," he said to Ramirez. "We can listen from here."

Sam drummed his fingers nervously on the steering wheel as he drove. He would normally blast some country rock to calm himself down, but he needed to be able to talk into the hidden mic if necessary. Plus, he didn't want to accidentally miss a call from Mullen.

He had to force his mind to stay focused and not wonder about the awful possibilities of what could be happening to Carla. Still, despite his best efforts, images of Mullen's previous victims flashed in front of him. The burn marks. The cuts. The wounds from where their wrists had been bound. His overactive imagination began to put together a picture of Carla's hands bound above her head, dangling in the air, a blindfold covering her eyes. Sam shook his head to shatter the image. He couldn't think that way. He needed to stay focused on solutions, not situations. This was his fault. He pulled Carla into this world, and she shouldn't have to pay the price.

State Highway 16 was a two-lane road that wound its way through the piney woods of East Texas. The winding road had no streetlights, making it difficult to see — especially when having to maintain the speed limit at all times. The sun was probably an hour and a half away from rising above the horizon, but it would start casting a blue gray glow over everything much sooner.

When his cellphone rang, it startled Sam so much he nearly swerved off the road. He answered it, making sure to put it on speakerphone so the mic would pick up the conversation.

"Where's Carla?" Sam asked.

"Well, aren't we Mr. Get Right To The Point?" Mullen teased on the other end of the line. "For now, she's fine. And she sends her best."

"Cut the crap, Mullen. Where do I need to go?"

"You're going to merge into 110 up ahead. Keep going west on it. Where are you now?"

Sam saw a traffic sign for the 110 merger.

"Almost there."

"Good. Right on time. And I see you're alone. That's good."

Sam looked around. Was Mullen close by? Watching him?

"I told you. I've got video cameras stationed all along the way, Big Guy," Mullen said, as if he could read Sam's mind. "I'm watching everything. Now, once you merge onto 110, I need you to keep your speed limit at 55. That way, I can track your progress. And Sam, no funny stuff. If I so much as suspect you're being followed or if you're not where you're supposed to be when I call back...well let's just say Carla may look slightly different the next time you see her."

"Just tell me where you are and stop playing games," Sam hissed.

"Oh, come on. I thought you more than anyone would appreciate a little playtime," Mullen laughed. "You're going to start getting serious on me now? You are on a need-to-know basis, Sammy, and right now, all you need to know is to get on 110."

"Let me talk to her."

"She can't come to the phone right now. Can I take a message?" Mullen teased before growing serious. "I'm not with her. I know your boys are going to try to trace this call, so I'm obviously not at our final destination. But she's doing fine. Nothing that won't heal."

Sam could feel the rage boiling inside him.

"I'm going to kill you."

"I really am so sorry it had to come to this, Sam," Mullen said. "You have to believe me when I say I truly appreciated our friendship. Let's not throw that all away."

"Go to hell, Ken."

Mullen hung up and Sam flung his phone to the passenger seat, exploding in anger and frustration.

7

6:00 a.m.

DESPITE HIS RAGE, Sam drove as instructed. He had driven nearly an hour and Mullen had called him three more times, taking Sam further and further off the beaten path. As the sun began to peek over the horizon, Sam came to a dead-end on a narrow blacktop road. Not sure what to do, he waited. Within a minute, Mullen called.

"Wanna guess which way to go?" he asked.

"Let's just get this over with," Sam snapped.

"I'm going to warn you. I haven't seen a single vehicle venture past this intersection so, if I do, I'm going to assume it's your FBI buddies. And that won't bode well for your dear Carla."

"I told you. I'm alone." Sam said, praying to God that Goldsmith had pulled back as he had promised.

"Well, now I need you to do one last thing before you come any closer," Mullen said. "I need you to take the tracker off your truck."

Sam feigned innocence.

"I don't know what you're talking about."

"There's no way the FBI let you drive out here without a tracker and you know it. You've got five minutes to find it and toss it. And I'm watching."

Sam looked around for possible video cameras but could find nothing obvious.

"When you find the tracker, I want you to hold it up in the air for me to see and then throw it in that field to your left. You have five minutes startinnnnggg now."

Sam got out of the truck, trying to remember where the agents had put the tracker. Goldsmith had been prepping him at the time, so he had been too distracted to pay much attention. He could remember that they never lifted the hood, which meant the tracker must be somewhere underneath the truck. Unsure of its location but very aware of the ticking clock, Sam got down on his hands and knees near the rear passenger tire and started feeling around the wheel house panel. Not finding anything but needing a better angle, he laid down on his back and shimmied underneath the truck. Fumbling along the surfaces of the axle and car frame, he ran his hand over every surface, squinting and spitting at the dirt and grime that fell on his face. Finally, as he felt around the front driver's wheel, he found something. A small round device the diameter of a quarter and half an inch thick. He pulled it off of the frame and pushed himself out from under the truck. Standing, he held the tracker above his head.

"Is this what you're looking for?" he yelled into the air, turning around in a circle.

He tossed the device far into the field, attempted to brush off the grime that covered his face and hands. His phone rang immediately.

"It's always the last place you look, isn't it?" Mullen said with a chuckle. "Alright. Now get rid of the other tracker they put on your clothes."

Sam's heart sank a bit. Sam set the phone down on the ground and felt around under his collar. He quickly found the tracker, ripped it out, and held it over his head before throwing it in the field as well. He picked up the phone again.

"Happy? Now, can we get on with this?" Sam yelled.

"Don't you feel better?" Mullen teased. "No secrets to weigh you down?"

"Why do this now? Why not when we started this wild goose chase?"

"I liked giving you a false sense of confidence. Now, just climb back in that god-awful truck of yours, take a right and follow the road for half a mile. Then turn left onto the gravel road that I've marked with an old stray sock."

Before Sam could say anything, Mullen hung up.

Sam followed Mullen's directions. As he drove, he spread the fingers to remove the concealed tracker. He had wedged it between his fingers before pretending to throw it. But now he wasn't sure what to do with it. Mullen would probably make Sam go on foot at some point so he couldn't hide it in the truck. And he would probably frisk him when they met. Left with few alternatives, Sam popped the small device in his mouth and swallowed hard.

Sam continued to get periodic instructions from Mullen that led him down a labyrinth of back roads, most of them unpaved, until he reached another dead end. He waited for another call, but his phone was silent. Then he noticed a piece of paper sticking out from under a rock. He got out of the truck to read it.

TIME TO WALK. FOLLOW THE GREEN Xs

Sam looked around for marks on any trees or rocks and finally spotted a small green X at the base of a large pine tree. He groaned. His frustrations had turned to anger as he thought about how much Mullen was enjoying this.

8

7:00 a.m.

Carla regained consciousness slowly and she struggled to make out where she was. Everything pressed in on her and she felt less like she was floating on air, but more like she was suspended in water. It was as if her brain was disconnected from her physical body. It would have been easy to fall back into the darkness. Let it swallow her back up again. But something in her wouldn't let her give up.

I've been drugged, she thought. *I need to fight it.*

Gradually, she pulled herself out of the slog. Everything was blurry and she couldn't hear a thing. Her body slowly began to respond, and she could finally lift her head. She could make out muffled sounds, but they seemed a million miles away. And she began to sense that someone was standing in front of her.

Then she felt the aching pain in her shoulders. Then a sharp pain in her wrists. Her arms were behind her back, but when she tried to pull them forward, she couldn't. Was her body still not cooperating with her mind?

Like an unwanted visitor, the reality of her horror began to emerge. She realized her wrists were bound together behind her back. She was sitting in a chair but when she tried to stand, she couldn't. She was tied to the chair as well. Her feet were also bound to the two front legs. Terror engulfed her and her breathing grew fast and labored as the person standing in front of her came into focus. It was Ken Mullen.

"Hello, Sunshine," he said in a sing-song voice.

Adrenaline pumped through her veins as she became increasingly conscious. She tried to yell at her captor, but nothing came out.

"Save your breath," Mullen said. "Your voice will come back soon enough. Can't rush Mother Nature! But I'll answer some questions I'm sure are racing through that drugged-up mind of yours.

"First, you're in one of my many work sheds. It's actually a cute little cabin in the middle of nowhere. No one around for miles. So you can scream and yell to your heart's content and no one will hear you. But I will probably tape your mouth shut.

"Your next question is 'What are you going to do with me?' That's a really good question and, I'll be honest, I don't rightly know. But I do promise I will enjoy it. And probably much more than you. You want something to drink?"

He took a slurping sip from a cup of coffee, then smacked his lips. Carla felt nauseous.

A common side effect of ketamine, she told herself.

Carla had performed an autopsy on one of Mullen's previous victims. She knew ketamine was his drug of choice. She also knew it could create a feeling of disassociation from the body, which explained what she was currently experiencing.

Carla struggled against the nylon rope binding her wrists, causing the chair to sway back and forth.

"I wouldn't fight so hard if I were you," he said. "It won't do any good."

He took another loud sip of coffee.

"Alright. Another question. 'Why are you doing this?' That's always a big one. For you, it's complicated. But most of the time, the answer's easy. To make the world a better place. To stop the suffering."

He tugged on the hem of the oversized blue T-shirt he had put on her.

"You like the shirt? It's the only clean one I had

around."

He pulled a stool over and sat down in front of her.

"The other women. You call them victims because of what I did, but you're looking at it all wrong. I freed them. They were victims long before I ever even set eyes on them. They were thrown out like garbage. Forgotten about. Forced to sell their bodies. Or addicted to drugs. They had dead-end, painful lives that no one deserves. And all those years in vice taught me one thing. There's no way out for those girls. You know as well as I do that you can't save them. I hated knowing what these women had to endure. And for what? Just to die early? So, I gave them mercy. Put them out of their misery. We do as much for animals, don't we?

"And I knew it wouldn't be seen that way. I knew short-sighted people like you and Sam would think I was some sort of monster. But I'm okay with that. Honestly. I know who I am. I know I serve a higher purpose."

As he spoke, he kept looking at his phone. Carla could see black and white video footage on the screen. Most likely a feed from some sort of surveillance camera outside. She tried to make out any details. There was an unpaved road that cut through low grass. The road looked lighter than the surroundings, so she deduced it was a limestone gravel. There were trees in the background. Cedars, maybe?

A few times Mullen had seen movement and looked more intently, but it was always an animal. A large dog? Sheep, maybe? Regardless, there were no cars and no people. Wherever they were, it seemed very remote.

"But why you?" he continued rambling. "You don't fit my typical victim profile. That's got to be rattling through that pretty brain of yours. And I truly hate it had to go this way. Sadly, you're just collateral damage in a much bigger game. And I whole-heartedly acknowledge that it's a petty game.

"I'm okay with people's misconceptions about me, but I see my old partner, your less-than-better half, getting rewarded for being half the man I am. He's too weak to do good. He let it break him. I watched him drink himself and his whole family away. He wasn't there for his son. He broke his wife's heart. Then he ran away from his responsibility to some small town. And suddenly he winds up getting hailed as the gift from the detective gods. You can see how that would upset me, right?"

Listening to him rationalize everything he had done was turning her terror into anger. Mullen noticed the fire in her eyes.

"You have something you want to say?" he asked with a smile.

She glared at him as she spoke, the words cracking out of her dry throat.

"You are so full of shit."

Mullen stiffened at the sound of her voice, but tried to hide his shock.

"If you're such an angel of mercy, then why do you torture them?" she asked.

Mullen opened his mouth to reply, but couldn't come up with an answer. He didn't want to tell her the truth, which was that he enjoyed it. That killing had become his addiction. Torture was like a drug to him. His victim's screams were the only sound that could quench the burning thirst that ate at him every day. He had managed to live a double life for decades, but the monster was always there.

But this self-righteous bitch had the nerve to question him?

He felt the familiar rage build. He grabbed a knife from the table behind him and thrust it in front of her face. She saw a rage ignite in his eyes as he glared at her.

"You best remember your place here," he sneered. "Or this will get unpleasant fast."

He stared into her eyes as he calmed down. A smirk cut across his lips and he lightly traced the knife along her cheek and to her neck. Then he quickly stood up, placed the knife on the workbench behind him, and rushed out of the room.

9

7:15 a.m.

SAM SWALLOWED his anger and got back to the task at hand: finding Carla. He grabbed his Glock 9mm and wedged it in the back waist of his pants. On the outside chance of an ambush, Sam needed to be ready.

He got out of the truck and trudged into the woods, scanning the terrain as he walked, taking in any detail that could help him find his way back. He figured he was walking east because the morning sun was glimmering low through the thick woods and right into his eyes. He tried to concentrate on his path but there was no path to follow, just an occasional tree marked with a small green X. The longer he walked, the more paranoid he became. Was Mullen watching him? Was he going to surprise him? Adrenaline buzzed through him and Sam pulled out his gun, finger on the trigger, prepared for Mullen to step out from behind a tree at any moment.

Sam spotted another note next to a green X. He opened it and read it quickly.

ALMOST HOME. TURN LEFT AT THE TREE AND WALK UNTIL YOU SEE IT.

Unsure of what "it" may be, Sam crouched as he walked. And walked. While it was only ten minutes, Sam felt like he had walked for hours and was beginning to wonder if he had gone in the right direction. He stopped to get his bearings and wipe the sweat from his forehead.

Sun's barely up and I'm already sweating, he thought.

Then he spotted something. The trees blocked enough of it for him to be sure, but it looked like there was a small log cabin up ahead.

10

———

7:20 a.m.

SAM CROUCHED LOWER and crept toward the structure in the woods. Once he was certain it was a cabin, he knelt to survey the surroundings. He knew he was being led into a trap, but if it meant it could save Carla, he didn't care. Still, he wasn't keen on going in on a suicide mission.

Mullen was surely watching him. Was he in the cabin? Or at some outside vantage point? He realized there was no sense in hiding. At some point, he was going to have to show himself. Mullen would either bring him in the cabin or he'd shoot him on sight.

"Damned if you do, damned if you don't," Sam grumbled as he stood.

"Lucy! I'm home," Sam yelled as he stepped casually into the clearing, fully exposing himself to anyone watching.

While he tried to look cool and calm, his heart was pounding in his ears and his breath had grown shallow and rapid. But with every step, the panic of thinking every breath he took could be his last soon melted into a kind of "it is what it is" Zen peace.

"Carla?" he yelled. "Are you in there?"

He heard no sounds from inside the cabin. The silence was unnerving. He stopped in front of the cabin door.

"Hello?"

There was no reply. Nothing. Suddenly, a different kind of panic swelled up inside of him. Was he too late? What was waiting for him on the other side of the door? He jiggled the door knob. It was unlocked. Holding his 9mm in his right hand, he pushed the door open with his left. It was dark, but Sam could make out a small unmade bed and a smaller bench. But other than that, it was empty. He stepped inside, confused, looking for any sign that Carla had been there. He looked for cloth-ing. For blood. Anything. But, other than the bed, there was no sign of life.

Then he heard the unmistakable click of a rifle's hammer.

"Who the hell are you?" an unfamiliar male voice asked.

Sam immediately put his hands in the air and turned around slowly. The barrel of a rifle was inches from his nose. At the trigger end of the gun was an old, disheveled man. His gaunt features were hidden behind a frazzled beard that engulfed everything on his face except for a wicked sneer.

"Put that baby gun of yours down on the floor," the man said. "Slowly."

Seeing no alternative, Sam carefully placed his gun on the floor and stood again, hands in the air.

"Now kick it on over to me," the old man said.

Sam did as instructed.

"Look. This is all just a big mistake. I must have the wrong house," Sam stammered. "Is this 1212 Crescent Avenue?"

"I could shoot you on the spot for trespassing."

"You could. But it'd make a helluva mess and then your whole day is wasted cleaning everything up," Sam replied.

The old man pushed the barrel of his gun into Sam's forehead.

"You got a smart mouth, boy," he said.

"I talk when I'm nervous," Sam said. "Bad habit."

The old man studied him, the gun still pressed against Sam's forehead.

"Get outside," he said.

Sam nodded and the old man kept his rifle trained on Sam as he led him back out of the cabin. Sam thought about telling the man that he was working with the FBI, but he had a feeling his new friend wouldn't react well to the mention of law enforcement.

"How'd you find me?" the old man asked.

"I didn't mean to," Sam decided to lie. "I got lost in the woods and saw the cabin. I just need directions."

"Who sent you? Who knows you're here?"

Sam was beginning to think this man was hiding from more than good hygiene. He weighed his answers. He could tell the man that there were other people with him that would show up soon and hope that would scare the man into letting him go. Or he could try to reassure him he was alone and was good at keeping secrets.

"Nobody knows I'm here," Sam replied. "I could walk away and never speak of this again."

"You're lying to me," the old man said. "You walked in with a gun."

"That? I can explain," Sam stammered as he tried to conjure up a good excuse.

The old man backed up, his rifle still trained on Sam. He reached around the side of the cabin to grab something. It was a shovel.

"Come on, boy. Walk with me."

""I'm kinda walked out, honestly," Sam asked.

"Shut up. We gonna dig a hole."

"Look. I'd love to help, but I really need to get going," Sam said, deciding to opt for a portion of the truth. "OK. Here's the truth. I am looking for someone. But not you. There's a bad guy. He's got my girlfriend. He's gonna kill her if I don't stop him."

The old man glared at Sam and finally grinned.

"That's a pretty good story," he said. "I like that one. Best one I heard yet. Now start digging."

11

———————

7:25 a.m.

MULLEN FLIPPED the pieces of bacon over as they sizzled in the cast-iron skillet. He inhaled deeply, taking in the intoxicating aroma. While he loved the taste of bacon, the smell of it cooking was probably even more satisfying. Same thing with coffee. Two perfect breakfast smells that filled him with so much happiness.

He glanced over at the surveillance video displayed on his phone to make sure Carla was still unconscious. He had a camera installed in the room where he kept her, as well as several others around the ranch. All viewable from his phone. As much as he hated so much of modern technology, there were things about it that were wonderful.

Carla was still tied to the chair, her head fallen forward. She wasn't moving, sedated by an injection of fentanyl. Mullen smiled at how peaceful she looked.

Normally, he wouldn't even have to keep an eye on her. He typically kept his victims sedated with ketamine. But that always came with a higher risk of them overdosing. For most women, that didn't matter. But he wanted to keep Carla alive a bit longer.

Mullen checked his watch and wondered if Sam had discovered the cabin and its paranoid owner yet. He chuckled to himself, imagining Sam's surprise when he not only didn't find Carla, but probably wound up at the long end of that old man's rifle.

I wonder if that old geezer shot him?

Part of Mullen would secretly love it if the old man had, but it would be a shame. There was so much he still had in store for Sam.

While Mullen imagined the panic that Sam must have felt when he realized he wouldn't be able to save his precious Carla, he pushed the bacon to the edges of the skillet and cracked an egg in the middle. The yolk immediately whitened and began bubbling. Mullen smiled as he thought about how pissed off Sam would be when he realized the last two and a half hours had been nothing but a distraction—and a reminder that Mullen had all the power.

He slid the eggs and bacon on to a plate which he sat on a small wooden table. But before he sat down, he walked over to a large tapestry that hung on a wall directly in front of the table. He pulled it aside to reveal a collage of pictures and newspaper clippings taped to the wall.

Mullen sat down at the table and admired his artwork as he ate his breakfast. There were several old pictures of Sam, back when he was a Houston cop. Old newspaper clippings that chronicled some of the honors he had been awarded. There was even one news photo of both Mullen and Sam together, back when they were partners. The collage also included some newer photos of Sam that Mullen had taken on the sly. Pictures of him leaving the police station. Working on his house. There were pictures of him laughing with Carla. And even the newspaper article announcing their engagement.

Mullen's eyes glanced from one image to another as he ate his breakfast. They began to have the effect that Mullen wanted. The stark reminders of all of Sam's successes made him angry. He was Sam's mentor, but Sam went on to shine. He helped Sam through his darkest days, but where was Sam when he needed him? He was getting his hands dirty. Making hard choices for the greater good. But Sam was off falling in love. How dare he?

Mullen's fury boiled. Sam didn't deserve happiness. Sam didn't deserve success. Sam didn't deserve love.

He hurled his plate across the room in a burst of anger. The plate shattered as it hit the wall of photos and Mullen seethed in his chair, glaring at the images of his old friend as egg yolk ran down over them.

12

7:30 a.m.

SAM DUG THE HOLE, working slowly in hopes that it would buy him enough time for the FBI to catch up to him. He prayed they would still be able to find him from the swallowed tracking device.

"So, you live here long?" he asked.

"Shut up," the old man snapped back.

"Just tell me. Was he even up here?" Sam asked. "I mean, do you know Ken Mullen? Big guy? Holding a woman hostage?"

"I'm tired of you talking."

"You've got to be hiding something around here. What is it?" Sam asked, ignoring the old man.

"I don't like strangers on my land."

"Still, burying them in your backyard is kind of extreme, don't you think?"

Sam stopped shoveling and turned to face his captor.

"How many other people are buried out here?" he asked.

"You talk too much," the old man sneered.

Sam chuckled.

"I get that a lot," he said.

"Shut up."

"I told you, I talk when I'm nervous."

"Shut up!" the old man yelled. "Listen."

Sam heard the faint sound of twigs and branches cracking. Someone was coming. Sam hid his sense of relief.

Finally.

The old man peered into the woods and saw movement everywhere.

"Shit," he said, turning his rifle around and pointing into the woods.

Sam took advantage of the distraction and swung his shovel to knock the rifle from the old man's hands. The old man looked down at the rifle, then glared up at Sam. Then he did something Sam wasn't expecting. He lunged at Sam. The two toppled to the ground. The old man was surprisingly strong for his age and immediately got the best of Sam, sitting on his chest and punching him hard in the face. Sam felt the bolt of pain ring through his skull.

"Jeez!" he yelled. "That hurt!"

The old man threw another punch, but Sam caught his hand and used the leverage to push him off. The old man rolled to the side and Sam scrambled to his feet, only to see the old man had wound up next to his rifle.

"Oh, come on," Sam yelled, as the old man stood.

Sam looked for a place to take cover, but they were in a clearing. He was a sitting duck. He closed his eyes and prepared for the worst.

"Freeze!"

The familiar voice of FBI agent Goldsmith came out of nowhere. Sam opened his eyes as a swarm of agents appeared out of the woods. The old man glared at Sam as he dropped the rifle and raised his arms in surrender.

"Oh, man. You should see your face," Sam said. "You look pissed."

Within minutes, over a dozen FBI agents and local law enforcement descended on the small cabin. As they scoured the area, they quickly found the reason for the old man's lack of hospitality. Not much further into the woods, hidden under a canopy of pine trees and camouflage netting, was a massive greenhouse filled with flowering Cannabis plants.

While the old man refused to speak, Sam suggested the officers check the woods for buried bodies. In less than a half hour, they had discovered three of them, all decomposed beyond recognition. Given the grave the old man was forcing Sam to dig, he felt sure the bodies were unfortunate hikers who had stumbled upon the grow site.

But more importantly to Sam, there was no sign of Mullen or Carla anywhere.

"I don't think they were even ever here," Goldsmith said.

"He was playing me the whole time," Sam growled. "So where are they?"

"Right now, we don't know," Goldsmith replied. "But don't worry. We were monitoring Mullen's calls. I think we got some pings from them."

"Then what are we waiting for?" Sam asked. "We need to be out there. She's out there somewhere!"

Goldsmith put a reassuring hand on Sam's shoulder.

"We're going to find her, Sam. I swear. But we can't be reactive. That's what he wants. We need to regroup and figure out a plan."

"Detective Lawson," a sandy-haired agent yelled from the cabin door. "You need to see this."

Goldsmith and Sam ran to the cabin and followed the agent inside to a small table. There was a small invitation-style envelope propped against a beer can. The name SAM had been handwritten on the front of it.

Goldsmith put on a pair of latex gloves and picked up the envelope.

"Uh, I believe that's mine, Goldie," Sam said.

Goldsmith watched helplessly as Sam snatched the envelope and opened it, pulling out a small notecard. He read it then turned to show it to Goldsmith.

8:00 P.M. TONIGHT was written across the top. Underneath it was a stick figure drawing of a woman with Xs for eyes.

13

9:30 a.m.

A GROUP of FBI agents and local police officers, constables and sheriff's deputies had squeezed into the briefing room at Quinton Police Headquarters, taking notes as Agent Goldsmith brought them up to speed.

"The wild goose chase Mullen led us on was obviously a ruse to buy time," he explained. "But we were able to roughly track his calls to give us a broad sense of where he's at."

He motioned to a tech agent who projected a map on a large monitor. There were several red pings on the map, designated where each call came from.

"Basically, while we were heading northwest, he was

heading southeast. And from the look of things, we have a pretty good idea where he's heading."

Goldsmith circled the town of Beaumont on the map. The pings all seemed to head directly toward it.

"Beaumont is Mullen's old stomping grounds. It's where he was born and raised. And where he first joined the force. He knows the area well and, chances are, has a hideaway spot in the area. In fact, he had inherited his parents' home, which is supposedly sitting empty. That's where we'll start our search."

"Doesn't that seem too obvious?" Sam asked from the back of the room.

Everyone turned to Sam, waiting for him to offer more. He was happy to oblige.

"Mullen's too smart to be that dumb," he said. "He knows we would have tracked his calls. Why would he lead us right to him?"

"Granted, it does seem easy," Goldsmith said. "But sometimes the simplest path is the right one. At the very least, it bears investigating. We know Mullen typically takes his victims to an undisclosed location. Sometimes, they are in close proximity to the abduction, but that hasn't always been the case. Maybe he has a preferred spot in Beaumont. We don't know how long he's been doing this, but we know it goes back awhile. That could mean his hometown would make sense."

Sam realized Goldsmith was looking at this as just

another abduction, but he knew different. For one, Mullen typically abducted women on the fringe of society - prostitutes, runaways, addicts. Women that wouldn't be missed for a while, if ever. Carla was a prominent member of the community. She was not only the county's chief medical examiner, she was connected with law enforcement. She couldn't be more visible.

Also, there were the events leading up to Carla's abduction to consider. Mullen had all but disappeared, only to reemerge months later in order to fake his own death. Originally, Sam assumed it was to quell any further manhunts, but Sam now realized he didn't fake his death to go off the grid. He did it so they would let their guard down, making it easier to grab Carla.

And then there was the note. 8:00 P.M. TONIGHT. Sam and Goldsmith both took it to mean the same thing. It was a deadline. They had until 8:00 this evening to find Carla or...

Sam looked at the office clock on the wall. Right now, it was 9:15 a.m. That gave them less than eleven hours to find her.

While Sam panicked over the ticking clock, Goldsmith was detailing a strategy involving two teams, one heading to Beaumont and a second heading to Houston, Mullen's last known residence.

"You're playing right into his hands," Sam protested.

"Look. I appreciate your frustration," Goldsmith said. "But to be perfectly candid, this is out of your wheelhouse. Apprehending serial killers is what I've been doing for fifteen years. You're going to have to trust me on this."

"You may know serial killers, but I know Mullen," Sam argued. "If he did things by the book, you would have apprehended him years ago."

Goldsmith sighed. He was trying his hardest to be patient, given Sam's relationship with Carla.

"We will proceed with this plan until we receive any information that dictates a change in strategy," he said firmly. "At the very least, we may uncover details that help us understand his motive better. That's going to be the key to tracking him down."

Sam started to protest, but Goldsmith spoke over him.

"I don't want to pull rank on you, Lawson. But you are a private citizen now. And one closely tied to this abduction. I'm giving you leeway by even allowing you in this briefing."

Sam started to argue but Goldsmith spoke over him.

"What we need you to do — what Carla needs — is for you to stay put in case he reaches out to you again."

14

———

9:45 a.m.

THE AGENTS and officers began to disperse, several of them stopping to assure Sam they'd get Carla back.

"She's part of our family," one detective said. "This is personal for all of us."

Sam half-listened. His mind was whirring, trying to figure out what to do. Goldsmith was right. He was just a private citizen now. His private detective license afforded him no special liberties. If he wanted to stay in the room, he needed to stay out of their way. At least for now.

So, he watched helplessly as they all strategized and planned their next move. One Sam was convinced was wrong. And, while Goldsmith had given him the task of "staying put in case Mullen called," he already knew that wasn't going to happen. There was no way he was just going to sit and wait. He just wasn't sure what to do.

As the officers filed out of the room, Sam noticed someone trying to push his way in.

"Sam!" the familiar voice said.

It was Josh Cole, the actor who was in town filming a Bigfoot movie. He had been shadowing Sam to prepare for his role as a detective and had proven himself to be a useful asset. He had even helped solve a murder just days before.

"I heard about Carla," Josh said. "Any news?"

Sam shook his head, not really feeling up to indulging the actor's false sense of their relationship.

"Carla's tough," Josh said. "I'm sure she's fine. And you found this Replacement Killer guy once. I know you will again."

Sam appreciated the shot of confidence.

"The set is still shut down while we regroup," Josh said. "What can I do to help?"

"I don't know," Sam said. "These guys are off barking up the wrong tree. I need to figure out a plan."

"Roger that," Josh said. "Heading to the bat cave?"

Josh was referring to the makeshift office in Sam's house where he had pulled together a wall of clues and evidence in his search for Mullen. And it was exactly where Sam was planning on heading.

"I need to figure this out," Sam said as he stood.

"I can help," Josh said. "Whatever you need."

Sam's first impulse was to turn the actor down. But now that he was on his own, having someone to bounce things off of could be helpful. And Josh did have good instincts.

He nodded at Josh, and they turned to leave, only to find Frank Bannon walking toward them. Sam's heart sank. Bannon was the chief of detectives and a major thorn in Sam's side. In fact, he was the primary reason Sam had unceremoniously quit the force and become a private detective. After that, Bannon had made Sam persona non grata at the police station and was no doubt here to kick Sam out of the building.

"I was just leaving," Sam said.

"You don't have to," Bannon said.

Sam couldn't recall the last time he had heard the chief speak to him without yelling, and he didn't quite know how to respond.

"Look. I know we've had our differences," Bannon said. "But I want you to know you have our full cooperation on this."

Sam could tell it was killing his old boss to swallow his pride like this, and he had to fight the urge to respond with a sarcastic comment.

"I appreciate that," he muttered instead.

"We're on top of this," Bannon continued. "Ramirez

is taking lead and you know he's our best. We will not rest until we find her."

Bannon, who had been staring at his feet as he spoke, looked up at Sam.

"Also, if there is anything I can personally do... well, know that I'm here."

Sam nodded. He realized it took a lot for Bannon to come to him, and it was greatly appreciated. But all Sam could think about was getting back to his house and focusing on the case. Bannon apparently picked up on Sam's restlessness.

"I know that look, Sam," Bannon said. "Remember. You're not a cop anymore."

Sam smirked. "Thank God."

Bannon's conciliatory mood shifted. "Alright. I'm trying to be nice here."

"No. You are being very gracious. And I appreciate it. I just meant... Mullen was a cop. He knows what cops can and can't do. I'm sure he's going to exploit that. I, on the other hand, don't have to play by those same rules."

Bannon nodded. He saw where Sam was heading.

"That's already more than I need to know," Bannon said.

Sam smiled.

"Go," Bannon said. "Call if you need anything."

15

10:30 a.m.

SAM AND JOSH walked past the forensic technicians that were still looking for evidence in Sam and Carla's house.

"There's beer in the fridge, boys," Sam yelled out as he led Josh past the kitchen toward his office. "Or coffee. Just help yourself to whatever you want."

Sam's "bat cave" was the spare bedroom that Sam had commandeered months ago in his original search for Mullen. He had disassembled the twin size bed and leaned the mattress and box spring side by side against the wall, creating an almost floor-to-ceiling bulletin board. A large map of Texas was pinned to the center of this Posturepedic Evidence Wall. Dozens of red pins marked the locations where Mullen's known victims were abducted. Red string connected these pins to a photo of the victim, along with any notes Sam had gathered about that specific murder.

To his left, the off-white wall that ran perpendicular to the mattresses was covered in notes written in black and red marker. Sam had apparently made the wall a mammoth dry erase board. Without the dry erasing.

"Carla must have loved that," Josh said.

"She balked at first," Sam replied. "But she caved quickly. Some of those notes are hers."

The only furniture in the 12x12 room was a couple of folding chairs and a folding table buried under a pile of files. On the far wall, maroon curtains covered a small window which, by the stale stench that had settled in the room, had clearly not been opened in a long time.

"That's everything I have on his murders. The place of abduction. The victims' names. Where their bodies were found. And this," Sam said, pointing to the other wall, "is everything I know about Mullen. His background. Where he's lived. Favorite color. Favorite food. Everything I could think of."

Josh whistled in admiration.

"This took a lot of work."

"The key to finding Carla is somewhere on these walls," Sam said. "Everything about how he took her deviates from his past abductions. He's never broken into a house. He targets women that are off the grid. And he doesn't contact their families."

"You stopped him before he killed his last victim, right?" Josh asked.

Sam had recently tracked Mullen to a cabin in the nearby river bottom. It was there that he had shot Mullen and watched him fall off a cliff, only to find out later that Mullen had faked the fall so he could more easily get to Carla.

"Even that was different," Sam said. "He left me clues. He wanted me to find him so he could fake his death. All of it is different. It's planned out in detail."

"What's his game?" Josh asked.

"I'll be sure to ask him that when I find him."

They studied the wall of clues, piecing together Mullen's story. He grew up in Beaumont, where Agent Goldsmith was currently heading. He was an average student but an all-star tight end on the football team. After high school, he joined the Army and became a decorated soldier. When he returned to Beaumont, he joined the police force. After a couple of years, he transferred to Houston. Was a beat cop for ten years, then moved into vice. After another six years, he was promoted to detective. A few years later, he was partnered with Sam. Mullen showed Sam the ropes and Sam regarded his partner as a mentor and friend.

"We hung out together. He came over for dinner all

the time," Sam recalled. "We even took vacations together. And he was always rock solid, through and through. Not me. The job ate me up. I started drinking. I lost my family and nearly lost my mind before Mullen helped me get the job here in Quinton. And for all I know, he was killing women the whole time. How could I not see it?"

"It's kind of scary what people can hide if they want to," Josh replied.

"I looked up to him," Sam said. "Maybe I was just too blind to see any clues."

"Maybe someone else saw him differently," Josh said.

Sam nodded. A light had gone off in his head.

"Yeah. I know someone. And he's not that far away."

16

II:3O a.m.

SAM AND JOSH knocked on Ed Kaster's door. They had phoned the ex-police chief on their way to his home in Big Creek, a small town about forty-five minutes south-east of Quinton.

Kaster opened the door immediately and, without saying a word, waved the two men to follow him inside. A short, burly man with a thick neck, balding head, and permanent scowl, Ed Kaster had been the Quinton Chief of Police, and Sam's boss, for years. But when Sam had inadvertently uncovered a cover-up that Kaster had orchestrated, the chief had voluntarily stepped down to avoid criminal charges. He had held a grudge against Sam but finally made his peace when

Sam solved the murder of Kaster's adult daughter. That's one thing about small communities. Stick around long enough, your enemies are going to turn into friends. And visa versa.

"Joyce is in the bedroom doing some sort of meditation crap," he made air quotes with his fingers. "Any updates since we spoke on the phone?"

"Nothing," Sam said.

"I guess no news is good news in a situation like this," Kaster replied.

"No news is no leads," Sam said.

Kaster led them into the kitchen and directed them to a small round table. A cardboard box was sitting on top of it.

"I made coffee," he said. "I'm guessing you've been up for a while."

The men sat down as Kaster poured them each a cup. Josh started to ask a question but Kaster cut him off, anticipating the question.

"I don't have cream or sugar," he said. "There's some milk in the fridge."

Josh nodded and quietly walked to the fridge.

"So why aren't you letting the experts handle it?" Kaster asked Sam.

"And just sit and wait?" Sam asked. "You, of all people, should know better than that."

Sam was referring to Kaster's knowledge of Sam's

personality, as well as Kaster's inability to sit on the sidelines while police searched for his daughter's killer.

"So what is this?" Sam asked, referring to the box in front of him.

"When I first heard about Mullen, I pulled this box down from the attic," Kaster said. "Momentos from when we were on the force together. I still can't believe Ken is capable of all of this."

"You kept scrapbooks?" Sam asked, unable to pass up an opportunity to tease his old boss. "That's so sweet."

Kaster ignored him, standing to open the box. He tossed a stack of photos in front of Sam.

"When Mullen came to Houston, I was his first partner."

Sam thumbed through the yellowed pictures of a young Kaster and a younger Mullen.

"Is that you?" Sam asked, pointing at the younger man with a full head of hair.

Kaster grabbed the photo out of Sam's hands.

"Ken was all fresh-faced and full of bravado," Kaster recalled. "He'd made a bit of a name for himself in Beaumont. But, that was a case of a big fish in a small pond. I think he was a little surprised when he didn't take Houston by storm. And working vice in a big city was an enormous culture shock for him."

"Any weird behavior?" Sam asked. "I mean, now that you have the benefit of hindsight."

Kaster shook his head.

"I have been racking my brains, trying to think of anything," he said. "I know it started to overwhelm him after a while. He was always talking about all those girls caught up in a terrible life. He tried to help them, but I warned him he shouldn't get involved. Couldn't get personal. But he didn't listen, and it eventually got to him. When he got promoted to detective and moved out of vice to homicide, it was just in time. He was on the verge of losing it."

"You think he could have been..." Sam asked the question without asking it.

Kaster shrugged.

"Killing already? Maybe. I don't know. But if he did, he sure hid it well. The Ken Mullen I knew couldn't do anything like that."

"Said every neighbor of every serial killer ever," Josh said.

Kaster looked at the young actor as he sat back down at the table.

"Who are you again?" he asked.

"He's helping me out," Sam answered. "So, did you keep in touch with Mullen after he moved to homicide?"

Kaster stared at Josh, trying to figure out why he looked so familiar. Giving up, he turned back to Sam.

"I did at first. But I had a wife and kid. Figured it was time to slow down. So I moved back to Quinton. We didn't talk too much after that. You know how it is. I probably hadn't heard from him in a couple of years when he called me out of the blue about you."

Mullen had reached out to Kaster and called in a favor to get Sam transferred to Quinton. Kaster was happy to help, but Sam's problem with authority eventually put a rift between the detective and his new boss. It had become an ongoing theme in Sam's career and why he eventually felt he'd be better off being his own boss.

Sam came across a picture of a group of cops. Mullen had his arm around a tall, skinny uniformed cop.

"Who's that?" he asked, handing the photo to Kaster.

"That's Cutter Moore. Mullen's old friend from Beaumont."

"He moved to Houston, too?"

Kaster nodded.

"They transferred to Houston at the same time," he said. "They had been Beaumont's dynamic duo. But Cutter didn't last long. This was at his going away party."

"Where'd he go?" Sam asked.

"Back to Beaumont, I think," Kaster said. "Man, Mullen was pissed. He took it really personally. Like Cutter had betrayed him."

"You know what happened to him?" Sam asked.

"He worked his way up the ranks. Became Beaumont's police chief. Although..."

His voice trailed off as he got up and left Sam and Josh alone in the kitchen.

"Where's he going?" Josh asked.

Before Sam could answer, Kaster returned with a laptop. He sat it on the kitchen counter and typed in a search. What he found seemed to confirm his thoughts.

"Says here on Beaumont's police site that Chief Robert "Cutter" Moore retired about eight months ago."

He read the rest of the article to himself, then shared his summary with his guests.

"I guess his wife passed on and he decided to call it quits. Says here he was going to go live with his son's family in... Tyler."

"That's thirty minutes from here," Sam said. "Does it give his son's name?"

"You can't just go dropping in unannounced at people's homes without a badge," Kaster reminded them. "Not everyone is as nice as me."

"Thank God for that," Sam said. "Never mind. We'll find it on our own."

"Hang on," Kaster groaned.

He read a bit more, then grabbed a piece of paper and wrote down a name. Sam was already standing when Kaster turned to hand it to him.

"Thanks, Chief," he said, already walking out of the kitchen. Josh pushed his chair back and followed.

"Nice meeting you," he said with a nod.

Kaster watched the two men rush out of his house. As soon as the door shut, Kaster realized where he had seen Josh before.

"Holy shit," he said out loud.

He turned and yelled down the hall.

"Joyce! You're not gonna believe who was just in our house!"

17

12:50 p.m.

GOLDSMITH STOOD in the backyard of Mullen's childhood home, drenched from an afternoon thunderstorm. He had long since given up on keeping himself dry. At least the rain had chased away some gawkers that had been camped out in front of Mullen's childhood home.

When Ken Mullen had first been identified as the Replacement Killer, the property had been inundated with reporters, curious neighbors, and true crime fans. Even though they were trying to keep the most recent developments of Mullen's re-emergence under wraps for now, Goldsmith knew it was only a matter of time before it leaked out. In fact, if their initial search didn't pan out, Goldsmith had every intention of going to the press to get the public's help in spotting the fugitive. But he knew that as soon as he did, Mullen would go into hiding and they would lose any element of surprise. He was gambling on his suspicion that Mullen had brought Carla back to his home turf.

The single-story ranch house had long been abandoned and was in a neglected state of disrepair. After Mullen's parents had died, the house had gone to their only son. But, even though Mullen had no interest in moving back to Beaumont, he never sold it. The house had sat empty for over a decade, isolated on several acres of land just outside of town.

In Agent Goldsmith's mind, that made it a perfect place for Mullen to bring his victims. With the help of the Beaumont Police Department, the federal agents did a quick sweep of the house and were now spreading out over the land behind it. Dan Russo, Beaumont's Chief of Police, grumbled with every step.

"I told you, we've already checked the property," he growled to Goldsmith.

"I'm sure you did, Chief," Goldsmith said, his eyes scanning the backyard and large field beyond it. "But he could've come back."

"We would have known," Russo replied.

Goldsmith decided not to engage any further. He

understood Russo's resentment. And the storm certainly wasn't helping to make things better.

The rain was coming down hard, making it difficult to see. The bark of search dogs echoed in the wet grayness, but the storm had most likely washed away any scent. Still, Goldsmith held his firearm at the ready, feeling certain they were on Mullen's trail. He couldn't deny the feeling of excitement that surged through him at the thought of capturing the notorious serial killer. The hunt for the Replacement Killer had been the chief focus of Goldsmith's time for over a year - long before they knew his identity.

But excited as he was at finally capturing his prey, Goldsmith's primary concern was stopping Mullen from killing Carla. Over the past few months, as he worked closely with Lawson to better understand Mullen, he had gotten to know the medical examiner. When he had first met Carla Davenport in her office, she came across as coldly professional and highly intelligent. It was only later, when he spoke to her outside of the office, that he began to really know her better. And although she always kept her guard up, she was friendly toward him. He could tell she was a strong woman and was sure she was giving Mullen hell.

"I know you're out here, you son of a bitch," he muttered to himself.

He was interrupted by the sound of the dogs barking more enthusiastically.

"Goldsmith! Chief! Over here!" an officer yelled from the distance.

Goldsmith and Chief Russo headed toward the voice, sloshing through mud puddles along the way. The officer stood next to a narrow, rushing stream of water at the bottom of a small ravine. The shallow water flowed from the house toward a large drainage tunnel that cut into a small hill. Normally, the water was little more than a couple of inches deep, but the runoff from the storm had raised the water level to half a foot, at least. The dogs were already in the tunnel, their barks echoing loudly. They had found something.

"We checked there already," Russo said. "It's just a drainage tunnel. Dogs are probably just excited to get out of this storm."

Goldsmith ignored Russo and quickly slid down the edge of the ravine to the creek's edge. He stepped into the shallow water and walked to the opening of the drainage tunnel, which only stood about five feet high. Goldsmith crouched in front of it, shining a flashlight inside.

"Whaddaya got?" he yelled to the agents already in the tunnel.

"You're gonna want to see this," one of them yelled back.

Goldsmith waded into the drainage tunnel, the rushing water hitting him mid-calf. Up ahead, two agents waited for him with their guns drawn and their German Shepherds barking and circling restlessly.

One of them used his flashlight to point at something on the side of the tunnel. At first, Goldsmith couldn't make out what it was. But as he got closer, it became clearer. A large rectangular outline marked where a portion of the metal tunnel had been cut away and repositioned as a door. Two deadbolts, one on either side, held it in place.

"We were here last week," Russo said. "That wasn't here before."

Goldsmith studied the door. It was old and rusty, but the deadbolts and hinges were new.

Knowing the barking dogs had already ruined any element of surprise, Goldsmith yelled back to the agents waiting at the tunnel's entrance.

"We're gonna need some bolt cutters. Now!"

18

1:00 p.m.

AFTER THE AGENTS cut the deadbolts, they carefully pulled the metal panel aside. The unmistakable smell of death immediately overtook them, and they all recoiled. Goldsmith grabbed a soaking wet handkerchief from his pocket to cover his nose and shined his flashlight into the dark space. From what he could tell, a small passageway quickly cut to the left. He motioned to the other agents, and everyone raised their firearms. A team of agents in full gear led the way, with Goldsmith and Russo right behind.

As Goldsmith expected, the passageway opened to a larger space, where the smell was even stronger. What they found was truly disturbing. The "room" appeared to be a natural cave. Mullen had probably discovered it at some point and turned it into his own private torture chamber. A large metal rack stood in the middle of the room. Hooks, chains, and nylon rope dangled from it. Goldsmith easily deduced it was where Mullen would hang his victims while torturing them. The dirt floor below the rack confirmed his suspicions. It was stained a dark crimson color. Blood, no doubt.

The entire cave was the size of a typical living room, but instead of a couch and chairs, it was furnished with a torture rack and a long, white folding table that sat against the far wall. An assortment of knives, pliers, and other "tools" were scattered over it. The thought of how they were used made Goldsmith's stomach turn. On the ground next to the table, a black duffle bag lay open. It was filled with duct tape, more canvas rope, and a couple of hammers.

Goldsmith shone his flashlight over the rest of the space, which was already filling up with agents. He knew by the smell that a body had to be somewhere. That's when he noticed the blue tarp balled up in a dark corner of the room. It could have been thrown haphazardly in a clump. Or it could be covering something. Goldsmith got one of the other agent's attention and motioned him toward the tarp. They both approached slowly, guns drawn. Standing over it, Goldsmith feared what he would find underneath, but knew there was only one way to find out. As he watched, his gun at the ready, the other agent yanked the tarp away with a single, swift jerk, releasing the pungent odor of decaying flesh.

"Jesus Christ," the other agent said.

Under the tarp was the body of a woman — or what had once been a woman — curled into a fetal position, facing away from the men. She was wearing nothing more than a T-shirt and a pair of underwear, both of which were covered in dirt, and what Goldsmith had to believe was blood. Her body had begun to bloat, and her skin had turned grayish-green. Her dark hair was dirty and matted with blood, hiding her face.

Goldsmith stood back to make room for a forensics team who had been at the ready for just such a gruesome discovery. He looked down at the corpse, guessing the victim had been dead at least a week. That meant it couldn't be Carla. Still. The hair color and body type were the same as Carla and it didn't take much imagination to realize this could soon be her fate if they didn't find Mullen soon.

"I swear to God that door wasn't here three days ago," Russo said. "I was down here myself."

"All this equipment has been here for a while, Chief," Goldsmith replied.

"I ain't saying it hasn't been," Russo countered. "But

that door is new. There's no way we could have missed that. And we would have noticed the smell."

Goldsmith came to two troubling conclusions. First, Mullen had replaced a concealed door with a more visible one just so it would be easier for them to find it. Second, he had moved a body here from a different location. But why? Was it to ensure his hiding place would be found? What purpose did that serve?

He looked around, exploring every inch of the room, taking in every detail and looking for any other secret doors or hidden passageways.

"This bastard's taunting us," Russo said.

Goldsmith nodded.

"He wants to keep us occupied," Goldsmith said quietly. "And we just played right into his hands."

19

1:05 p.m.

CARLA'S EYES darted around the room, looking for any way she could free herself. Mullen was nowhere in sight and she didn't hear him in another room. She had no idea what time it was or how long she had been knocked out.

She had noticed that she had felt differently when she regained consciousness this time. He must have injected her with something else. Probably fentanyl. And probably because he didn't want to risk an overdose. Based on what she knew from police records, and her own autopsy of one of the victims, it was a consideration he didn't normally offer. In fact, his previous victims had suffered immeasurable abuse and torture.

So far, he had done none of that to her. Was she being treated different for a reason or was he just saving it?

She blinked her eyes, trying to clear them of the tears that were streaming down her cheeks. She felt the panic start to rise in her chest, but knew she needed to find the strength to push it back down. Panic would do her no good. She needed to stay focused. She took long, deep breaths and felt herself start to calm down.

She stared at the knife he had placed on the workbench earlier. Even if she was able to get to the bench, she wouldn't be able to reach the knife. She looked around the room for some other possible way to escape.

It was a small room. The walls and floor were unfinished wood and a door to her left separated her quarters from the rest of the cabin. She had no idea what was out there. The door was typically shut and Mullen made sure to slip in and out quickly so she couldn't get a glimpse beyond her room. But from the sound of his footsteps, it didn't seem that large.

Then something caught her eye on the floor under the workbench. It was a different, smaller knife that must have fallen off the table.

If I can get to it, I may be able to cut myself free.

She rocked her chair side to side. If she could topple the chair on its side, she could shimmy across the floor. Even bound to the chair, she would be able to grab the knife.

Her heart raced. It was a long shot and she was fearful of what would happen if Mullen appeared. But it was probably her best chance at survival and she knew she had to take the risk.

She gulped and was prepared to go for it when the sound of approaching footsteps stopped her. Mullen opened the door, quickly shutting it behind him.

"Well, someone's all awake and alert!" he chimed, holding up a glass of water. "I figured you must be parched."

He pulled the stool in front of her and sat down, holding the glass up to Carla's lips. She quickly turned her head to the side.

"You think I'd poison you?" he asked incredulously.

He took a gulp of water from the glass to prove it was safe.

"See? Nothing to fear."

He brought the glass to her lips again. This time she reluctantly parted her lips and drank, staring Mullen in the eyes the entire time. Mullen smiled and placed his free hand under her chin to catch the dribbles of water that ran down her mouth.

"I can see the fire in your eyes," he said as he pulled the glass away. "You still have hope, don't you?"

He gave her another sip.

"But Sam's not gonna save you," he continued. "He's

not smart enough to find us. All he is, and all he has ever been, is lucky."

Mullen took the glass away and drank the rest of it himself.

"How do you think he wound up with a lady like you?" he continued. "You're way out of his league, if you don't mind me saying so."

"You can't hold a candle to Sam," Carla spit back.

Mullen smiled.

"He's not the knight in shining armor you think he is. He's an alcoholic and a screw-up and eventually destroys every good thing that happens to him. I've seen it with my own two eyes."

"I know about his past," Carla replied. "I know about his old family. About his son. I know he struggled. And I know you helped him out of it."

"Mullen to the rescue, once again," Mullen said. "He's a losing horse, Carla. You shouldn't have put your money on him. I don't want you to die without knowing that."

20

1:20 p.m.

THE FRONT DOOR of the Moore's home swung open before Sam could even knock. Jim Moore stood in the doorway, scowling at his unexpected visitors. Standing next to him was his wife, Rhonda. She looked right past Sam to Josh.

"Oh my God, it's really you!" she exclaimed.

When Sam called in advance, Rhonda had fortunately answered the phone. He immediately played the "I-have-the-star-of-all-your-favorite-romantic-movies-with-me" card. Josh played along, taking the phone from Sam and speaking to the star-struck woman. She eagerly invited the two to her home, asking only that she be given enough time to get dressed. Now she greeted them at their door — full make-up on, hair combed, and dressed in a black cocktail dress. Her husband Jim was wearing a T-shirt and jeans – clearly not as enthused by their movie star meeting.

"You say you're with the Quinton police?" he asked suspiciously. "You got a badge?"

"I may have kind of misspoke," Sam said. "I WAS with the Quinton police. Now I'm a private detective, but I'm WORKING WITH the Quinton PD and the FBI on this case."

He handed Agent Goldsmith's business card to Jim.

"You can call to confirm," Sam said.

As Jim studied the card, Rhonda pushed him to the side.

"Jim, don't be so rude," she said, ignoring Sam and extending her hand to Josh. "Please. Come inside."

Josh rewarded her with his famous smile and a squeeze of her hand as she led him into the house.

"Thank you so much, Rhonda. That's a beautiful dress."

Rhonda looked down at what she was wearing and began to feel a little silly for getting so dolled up.

"Well, I had to throw something on. This was just lying around."

"Dad's in the living room," Jim said, walking quickly to stand between Josh and his wife. "Follow me."

Sam and Josh followed the couple down the short

hallway. Family photos adorned the walls, but Sam barely noticed them. His eyes were focused on the man sitting on a couch in the living room. Robert Moore, known as Cutter to just about everybody. He was a frail-looking man with thin lips and a hooked nose. His silver hair was cut so short that his pink scalp shone through. And, even though he had to have been the same age as Mullen, he looked years older.

Cutter stared at Sam as the group walked into the room, and Sam could tell he was sizing him up. They had both been partners with Ken Mullen, which Sam had hoped would foster some sort of kinship. But he could see the suspicion in the old man's eyes. While Josh was being held hostage by Rhonda's desire for pictures and Jim was busy keeping his wife from completely throwing herself at the actor, Sam walked to Cutter.

"Mr. Moore, so great to meet you. Sorry about the last-minute drop-in."

Cutter shook his hand, squeezing a little harder than usual.

"It's okay. I know the job," Cutter said.

Sam sat down next to Cutter and caught him up to speed on everything that had happened in the past 24 hours.

"I still don't know how I can help you," Cutter said.

"Honestly, I don't either," Sam replied. "I'm kind of

grabbing at straws. Looking for some sort of miracle. I need to find anything that can help me figure out where Mullen has taken Carla."

Cutter raised his hand and nodded. He didn't need a full explanation.

"Ask me anything," Cutter said. "I'll do my best to answer you."

Sam asked him about working together for the Beaumont Police Department.

"Is that when you met?"

Cutter laughed. He was starting to let down his guard a bit.

"Oh, we go back way further than that," he said. "Ken and I were friends since we were rug rats. We were joined at the hip from grade school on. Even went through the police academy together."

"And then you were both cops in Beaumont," Sam said.

"Yes, sir. Partners."

"And then he wanted to move on to bigger things. To Houston."

Cutter laughed again.

"Oh, hell no. I'm the one that got restless. He'd have been happy handing out parking tickets for the rest of his life. I had to convince him to come with me and take on the big city. We were naive enough to think we could still be partners. But Houston's too big to cater to the needs of two cock-sure, small-town cops. But even though we worked in different precincts, we stayed close. Until I got married and we moved back home."

"Back to Beaumont?"

"Mean streets get meaner when you got something to lose. You know what I mean?

Sam nodded. He knew all too well.

"Ken was pissed at me. Can't say I blame him much. I asked him to come back to Beaumont with me. But by then he was a shooting star in Houston. He took to the big city like a duck to water. Felt like he was making a difference. At first, anyways. But, like I said, after I moved, he kind of lost touch. I guess I did, too."

"So, there were no signs of... all of this stuff?" Sam asked.

"You were his partner, too. Did you see any signs?"

Sam shook his head and the two men sat in an uncomfortable silence while Sam tried to think of another question. He studied Cutter's face and got the feeling that the old man wanted to tell him something but wasn't sure if he should. Then Sam saw his face change. Like he had talked himself out of it.

"Guess he learned to compartmentalize it," he said.

Sam nodded.

"Yeah. I never was good at doing that."

"Me neither," Cutter said. "That's why you got out, too. Right? I wish Ken would've done the same thing.

Maybe he wouldn't have gone off the deep end. I still can't believe everything I'm hearing about him."

"Mr. Moore, is there any place you know of where Mullen would have taken Carla?"

Cutter seemed so deep in thought, Sam wasn't sure if he had heard the question. Finally, Cutter spoke.

"Funny thing happens when you get old. I guess some people learn to live with their regrets. Other people just double down."

"Sir? Do you have any idea where they could be?"

Cutter snapped himself back to the moment. He thought for a second. Sam wasn't sure if he was trying to remember a place, or debating whether to tell Sam. Finally, he shook his head.

"I'm sorry I'm not much help to you," he said, standing to signal the end of the conversation. "But if I think of anything, I'll definitely give you a call."

Sam also stood, but he still had one more question.

"Sir, has Mullen tried to contact you lately?"

Cutter stiffened. The question hit him like a slap across the face.

"Don't you think I would have told you if he had?"

It was clear he was offended, but Sam didn't stop.

"It's just that... given your past and all, I thought he'd maybe..."

"You have a past with him, Mr. Lawson," Cutter snapped. "Has he tried to contact you?"

Sam had been teetering on the edge, trying to remain calm and civil while hiding his panic and frustration. Cutter's hostile tone was all it took to push Sam over.

"Yeah. As a matter of fact, he did contact me! By kidnapping my girlfriend. And now he's threatening to kill her. So don't you go and get all indignant on me, old man!"

"Get out!" Cutter yelled, pointing toward the door.

Cutter's son Jim stepped in.

"I think y'all better get going."

"You come into my house and accuse me of withholding evidence?" Cutter yelled. "I've got friends in high places, boy. You don't want to mess with me."

Sam started to argue back, but Jim quickly escorted him to the door.

Josh peeled himself away from a very clingy Rhonda to run after him. As they walked to Sam's truck, Josh nudged Sam and asked how it went.

"He's holding something back," Sam said.

"Sure didn't sound like he held back to me," Josh replied.

"I don't know if he's protecting Mullen or just in denial. But he got way too defensive, way too quick. Something ain't right."

21

1:30 p.m.

"You alright, Dad?" Jim asked.

The question snapped Cutter out of his thoughts. He forced a smile and looked up at his son.

"That detective just got me riled up," he said. "I'm fine."

"He was definitely annoying," Jim said. "You want some lunch?"

Cutter stood up with a groan.

"I ain't that hungry," he said. "I may go do a little puttering in the shed to help me calm down."

"Sure you don't want me to make you something?" Rhonda asked.

Cutter waved her off.

"Nah, I just need to wind down. A little me-time in my office will do the trick."

Rhonda kissed Cutter on the cheek.

"You take all the time you need."

"I should get back to work," Jim said to his wife.

"You didn't have to come home on my account," Cutter said.

"Don't flatter yourself," Jim winked. "I wasn't about to let some movie star come visit my wife without being here."

Rhonda playfully hit him with a throw pillow and the two kissed.

Cutter watched the couple flirting with each other and let out a deep sigh as he shuffled into the kitchen and out the back door. It opened to a brick path that led to a separate one-car garage. Years ago, Cutter had taken up the hobby of woodworking to help him relax. In fact, he had become quite good at building handmade wooden chairs, stools, and tables. After Cutter's wife died, Jim was insistent that his dad move in with him and his family. Cutter was reluctant at first, but Jim sweetened the pot by offering to convert the garage into a woodworking space. It did the trick. Cutter agreed to move in but insisted on paying rent and chipping in for groceries. Knowing it was a matter of pride for Cutter, Jim accepted the money. But they would have happily paid him for all he did.

Cutter had quickly proven himself to be a big help in the Moore household, primarily in watching Jack, their six-year-old son. Jim worked full-time, and Rhonda picked up random shifts at a local plant nursery. Having Cutter at home after school was much better than hiring a babysitter or finding an after-school program for their son.

Cutter pulled a key from his pocket and unlocked the side door to the garage, flipping on the work light as he entered. He looked back to make sure no one had followed him and then walked over to his workbench, kneeling down to a red toolbox on a lower shelf. The toolbox was heavy, and it took all of Cutter's strength just to push it a few inches to the side. But that was just enough to allow him to reach behind it and lift a panel of insulation attached to the wall. He fumbled around in the space behind the insulation until he found what he was looking for. An old tin cigar box.

He set the tin box on the worktable, once again checking to make sure no one was watching. The sides of the box had been duct-taped shut. Not so much to hold the lid down, but so he could tell if anyone had tampered with the box. He peeled off the gray strips of tape and carefully removed the lid. The box was filled with an odd assortment of mementos. An old police badge. Some crumpled newspaper clippings. And a pile of nondescript postcards. Cutter pulled the postcards from the box and slowly rifled through them. They had no images on them and, other than his name and address, very few words. Sometimes, an exclamation point. Sometimes just a number. They would mean nothing to anyone that came upon the postcards, but they meant a lot to Cutter. As he looked through them, tears welled up in his eyes. His lower lip trembled, and he took a deep breath to collect himself.

Cutter had started receiving them shortly after he had moved back to Beaumont. At first, Cutter didn't know what to make of the cryptic, anonymous cards, but he recognized the handwriting. They were definitely from Mullen. Then a few bodies started turning up around Houston. Call it a cop's gut feeling or a paranoid hunch, but Cutter began to fear that Mullen was sending him a postcard every time he killed someone.

Cutter had tried to confront his old friend, but Mullen refused to talk to him. He just kept sending the cards. And every time he did, Cutter was filled with a renewed sense of dread and guilt. He would scan the local papers for reports of missing women or Jane Does that had been discovered.

For years, Cutter carried the weight of these postcards. He never told anyone. Mullen was like a brother, for God's sake. He would rationalize that 'this would be the last one'. But the cards kept coming. Women kept dying.

And Cutter did nothing.

As it is with all lies, they become heavier the longer you carry them. After a while, Cutter had a new reason for not telling anyone about the cards. He knew he'd be held accountable for withholding evidence. The guilt he carried was now coupled with a sense of dread that he carried every day. And after Sam's visit, he felt it pressing in on him from all sides.

He threw the postcards back in the box and slammed the lid back down, grabbed a roll of duct tape and created a fresh seal around the box's edge. Then he carefully placed it back in its hiding place.

What have I done?

He held on to the table to steady himself as the weight of the lies dug into him. Meeting Sam and seeing his pain was like throwing a match on gasoline. How many women died because he kept this awful secret? Now there's a coroner who has been kidnapped. A man suffering as he searched for her. He could have prevented all of it.

He looked at a framed picture of himself and his wife and forced a weak smile.

"I'm so sorry, my love," he muttered.

While he'd never told anyone his secret, today was the first time he had to lie about it. It cracked the wall of denial he had so carefully built up over decades. It was all crashing down on him and he was the only one who could feel the weight.

He couldn't carry this lie any longer. But he could never tell the truth. There was only one way out.

He took another deep breath and reached up to a small safe on the top shelf. He slowly and carefully entered a combination, then opened the safe door, pulling out a black SIG Sauer handgun. He opened a smaller toolbox on the table and grabbed a box of 9mm ammo. His hands shook as he loaded the gun's clip, tears streaming down the lines on his face.

He snapped the clip into the gun and closed his eyes to gather his strength. A steely resolve overtook him as he pulled the slide back and loaded a single round into the firing chamber. Then, staring at his wife in the picture, he pointed the gun under his chin.

22

1:35 p.m.

SIX-YEAR-OLD JACK WALKED INTO HIS PARENTS' bedroom just as Rhonda finished changing out of her black cocktail dress and back into her normal daytime wear of jeans and a T-shirt.

"I can't find Grampy," Jack said.

"Hey, buddy. Grampy's in his shed right now," Rhonda answered. "Can I help you with something?"

"I'll go get Grampy," Jack replied, walking out of the room.

Rhonda ran after him and stopped him in the hallway.

"I think Grampy needs a little alone time."

"Why? Did he get in trouble?" Jack asked.

Rhonda laughed.

"No. He didn't get in trouble. Sometimes grown-ups just like to be alone."

"Do you like to be alone sometimes?"

Rhonda laughed again.

"I don't even remember what alone time is. Come on. I'll make us some lunch."

Jack followed her into the kitchen and sat at the table, watching his mom gather sandwich supplies. Before she could even set the bread down on the kitchen counter, her phone rang in another room. Rhonda hurriedly wiped her hands on her jeans and rushed out of the room. Growing restless, the six-year-old decided his grandfather's alone time surely didn't include Jack. He was always glad to see him.

Jack opened the back door again and walked to the garage. He turned the doorknob, but it was locked.

Why would Grampy lock the door? Jack wondered.

He grabbed a nearby plastic lawn chair and dragged it in front of the door, climbing up on it to look inside the door's window. He had barely cupped his hands in front of his face to look inside when a loud shot rang out.

23

3:00 p.m.

NOT KNOWING what to do next, Sam and Josh retreated to Sam's house and his mattress wall of clues. Sam scrawled Cutter's name on the wall that doubled as a giant notepad.

"He knows something," Sam said. "I need to talk to him again."

"I don't think he's going to be so quick to agree to another interview," Josh said. "Maybe give him a little time."

"We don't have the luxury of time," Sam snapped.

Josh knew better than to respond. He sat back on a stool and watched Sam pace back and forth, muttering under his breath, until he finally turned his attention to the Texas map pinned to the mattresses.

"How much time do we have?" Sam asked.

"About five hours."

"We're missing something! Where would he take her?" he asked out loud.

"Some place close?" Josh asked. "A place of opportunity."

Sam thought about it, then shook his head.

"Then he wouldn't have needed to throw us off course," Sam said. "He was buying time. But why did he need time?"

He walked closer to the map.

"He needed time to get somewhere. That rules out anything within a one-hour radius."

"That still leaves most of Texas," Josh said.

"No shit."

Their thoughts were interrupted by Sam's cell phone. Sam pulled it out of his pocket and looked at the screen. His shoulders dropped in disappointment.

"It's Ramirez."

He answered the phone.

"Whaddaya got?"

"What the hell, Sam?" Ramirez yelled. "What did you say to him?"

"Say to who?" Sam asked.

"Cutter Moore. You've got no business going to his

house saying you're working with the FBI and stirring shit up!"

"I thought he might know something. I still think he does."

"Well, you won't find out now. As soon as you left, he put a gun to his head."

"What?" Sam asked.

Josh stood up. He could tell from Sam's expression that it wasn't good news.

"According to his son, right after you and that actor friend of yours left, he went out to the garage and shot himself. The only reason he's not dead is because his grandson distracted him just as he was pulling the trigger. He must have jerked just enough to throw the bullet off its path. It wasn't a fatal shot, but it still put him in a coma."

"Jesus," Sam said.

"What did you say to him?" Ramirez asked.

"I just asked him about Mullen. He kicked us out before it went anywhere."

"Well, you must have said something," Ramirez said. "His family is pissed and I'm sure they're lawyering up."

"I don't have time to care about that," Sam replied. "My gut was telling me Cutter was hiding something and now I'm even more sure. I need you to get a warrant to search his place."

"On what grounds?" Ramirez shouted. "You need to let Cutter go. For your own good. Also… Goldsmith stumbled on something in Beaumont."

Sam could tell by the change in Ramirez's voice that it wasn't good.

"Some hidden torture room," Ramirez continued. "There was a body inside."

Sam's heart dropped to his stomach.

"But it's not…" Sam couldn't even ask the question.

"God, no. It's not Carla," Ramirez said. "Jesus, don't you think I would have led with that? It's a Jane Doe. Been dead over a week."

Sam let out a sigh. The sense of relief was pulling up a well of emotions that Sam did not feel like sharing.

"It's got his M.O., though. Earring missing. The whole nine yards. But there was some weird stuff. It was like he wanted us to find her."

"Another distraction. So, what's Goldsmith doing now?"

"They got another bite in Houston he's checking out."

"Goldsmith is playing right into Mullen's hands. Don't you see what he's doing? He's trying to tie up as many officers as he can for as long as possible."

"That's what Goldsmith thinks, too. But he doesn't have any better leads and has to follow through. Just in case."

"He's wasting time," Sam snapped. "Mullen is nowhere near Houston."

"You have any better ideas?" Ramirez asked.

"I will," Sam said as he hung up.

He looked up at Josh.

"We've got to get back into Cutter's house."

Josh badgered Sam with questions as he followed him out of the room, past the agents, and to the front door. Sam swung the door open and stopped cold.

Standing on the other side was an attractive, well-dressed woman and two sloppily dressed men. Sam recognized the woman immediately. She was a news journalist, Nancy Hellard.

24

____

3:05 p.m.

"I DON'T HAVE time for this," Sam said abruptly as he pushed past the reporter and her two companions.

"Is it true? Is he back?" Nancy said. "I got over here as fast as I could."

"I bet you did," Sam growled. "I can see you haven't changed a bit."

Nancy Hellard used to be an ambitious young reporter for the local Quinton TV station who had quickly made a name for herself, primarily from helping to break one of Sam's cases. She had since become a reporter for the True Crime Channel and even had her own show, _To Kill Again_, which focused on serial killers.

"I only came to confirm what I've heard. And to see how you are doing," she answered.

Josh wasn't as quick to dismiss the reporter and the two men, who were now clearly carrying a camera and a boom mic. He figured the press could help spread the word and assumed Sam did, too. He was surprised when Sam turned on the reporter.

"Oh? You're suddenly so caring?" he asked. "I suppose your boys here are with Hallmark?"

"The story is going to break. Don't you want to be on top of it when it does? I thought you might want to share some information so I could help get the word out. I have a large audience," Nancy said. "I met Ms. Davenport. I want to help."

"You want a scoop," Sam said. "Don't bullshit a bull-shitter."

"Sam, maybe she could help," Josh interjected.

Nancy and her crew turned toward Josh for the first time and were instantly confused by his recognizable face. The lightbulb went off with the camera operator first.

"You're that guy," he muttered.

Nancy now made sense of the familiarity, too.

"You're Josh Cole," she said.

The camera operator snapped his fingers and pointed at Josh.

"You're in those TV movies!"

Josh nodded.

"I work with Sam sometimes," he said, further confusing the news team.

Sam decided to let them stay confused.

"Actors are okay," he said. "It's reporters I don't trust."

"The more his face is planted everywhere, the greater the chance he'll be seen," Nancy said, returning to the subject.

"And the greater the chance he'll feel cornered," Sam added. "That's what we want to avoid. Please."

"I can't sit on this story forever, Sam," she said. "If I don't break it, someone else will."

"I need you to sit on it as long as you possibly can," Sam replied. "And ask your other media vultures to do the same. I don't have a lot of time and I don't want to escalate things."

"So, he's given you some sort of deadline?" she guessed. "For what? He has demands?"

Sam ignored her as he climbed into his truck.

"Move your news van or I'll run it over," Sam said.

Realizing she wasn't going to get anywhere with Sam, she turned to Josh.

"Please talk some sense into him," she said. "I just want to help."

"Give me your number," Josh said. "I promise I will call you. I can't guarantee a scoop, but I can guarantee you'll have first shot at me. Linking a celebrity to this case has got to be better than just being the first one to break it by an hour or two."

Nancy scrambled for a business card and thrust it at Josh. "You promise me."

Josh nodded. "On my mother's grave."

Sam honked the horn from inside the truck.

"We really do have to go," Josh said. "Please don't follow us. I promise I will call."

Nancy reluctantly nodded.

"As soon as you can," she said.

Josh nodded and jumped into the passenger seat of the truck. Nancy turned and directed her crew to their van that was parked behind Sam's truck.

25

4:00 p.m.

SAM'S TRUCK sat under a large sweetgum tree down the street from the Moore home. Nancy appeared to stay true to her word and hadn't followed them.

"This is a really bad idea," Josh said as he hung up the phone.

"It's only a bad idea if we get caught," Sam replied.

As they had raced back to the Moore's house, Josh had called to confirm the entire Moore family was still at the hospital.

"You can't just break into their house," Josh argued.

"It's not like I'm robbing them," Sam said.

"Why don't you call Ramirez? Get a warrant or something?"

"Because, Nit-brains, no judge would grant a warrant without just cause."

"Exactly why you shouldn't be doing this."

"Since when did you become my lawyer?" Sam asked.

Josh didn't answer. He could tell that Sam wasn't going to change his mind.

"You didn't have to come with me," Sam reminded Josh.

"Someone's gotta watch your back," Josh replied. "Hurry. If you're gonna do this, do it."

"I love it when you worry about me," Sam said with a wink. "Text me if you see anything."

Sam walked up the street as inconspicuously as possible, keeping his head low to hide his face from nosy neighbors. When he reached the house, he made a beeline up the driveway toward the side door to the garage. Police tape had been stretched across the door, but, since there had been a witness – and Cutter was a former police officer – any investigation had wrapped up quickly.

Sam removed his trusty lock pick from his back pocket and quickly jimmied the door open. Not wanting to turn on the light or use a flashlight as it may draw attention, he stood in the darkness, waiting for his eyes to adjust. Hopefully, the sunlight seeping in from the garage door windows would give him enough light to see. At first, all he could make out was the darkest contrasts, which included the blood that covered the floor and desk. Once he could see better, he walked to the bench, being careful not to step in anything. He scanned the bench top and the shelves, looking for anything that could be useful - a hard feat, considering he wasn't even sure what he was looking for.

He opened drawers and rifled through the tall toolbox that sat to the side of the workbench. Still coming up empty, he turned his attention downward. That's when he saw the smaller toolbox on the shelf. Blood had pooled directly in front of the toolbox, making it difficult to reach, so Sam grabbed a shovel and clumsily pawed at the toolbox's latches, pushing the toolbox to the side. Finally, he was able to open it but, once again, found nothing but tools. Then he noticed the scratch marks under the shelf where the toolbox had been sitting. At first, he assumed he had made them while moving the toolbox around. But there were too many of them and most of them seemed to have been there for a while.

Sam crouched to see what was behind the toolbox and was disappointed to find nothing but insulation. He stared absentmindedly at it, trying to figure out his next move, and noticed something slightly odd. The panel of insulation wasn't tucked in the way the other panels were. It was a long shot that it meant anything, but it was the only shot Sam had. He grabbed the shovel again and used it to pull the insulation up, then tapped around the space. His efforts were answered by the sound of something metal.

Sam knew he couldn't pull the mystery object out with the shovel and he couldn't reach it without stepping in the blood. His eyes darted around the garage, looking for something to help him. On the back wall of the garage, cardboard boxes were stacked high to the ceiling. He noticed something sticking out of one of the open boxes and he smiled. It was a set of fireplace tools.

Sam grabbed the poker and got on his hands and knees, leaning on one arm and stretching with the other as far as possible to reach the insulation. His left arm shook under the weight of his body as the right arm used the poker to grab whatever was hidden in the wall. He knew that, if his arm gave out, he would fall flat right in the middle of the pool of blood. Sam groaned, mustering all of his strength as he moved the poker around. Finally, it felt like he found a handle. Gently, he lifted the mystery object out of its hiding place. With a loud grunt, Sam pushed up and away, accidentally hurling the metal box over his head and against the wall behind him.

Sam took a second to catch his breath, rubbing his

overworked arm. Then he turned his attention to the tin box lying next to him. He broke the duct tape seal and took off the lid, turning so the sunlight shone down on the contents. On top of everything was the stack of postcards.

Why would Cutter save these?

He examined the cryptic messages: A number. An exclamation point. One of them contained a complete sentence: "This one was for you."

Sam studied the handwriting on the note. It looked familiar. Part of him wanted to believe it was Mullen's handwriting, but he knew that was probably just wishful thinking on his part. Still, he removed a folded piece of paper from his wallet. It was a copy of the threatening note Mullen had sent him after he had first escaped. Comparing it to the postcard, his heart raced. He wasn't crazy. It was a match.

So, Mullen had been sending postcards to his old friend. Some were sent ten years ago. One was dated three months ago. He studied them. Looking for anything that could be a clue.

Then he noticed the postmark.

He rifled through the postcards, noting the postmark on all of them. They all were sent from the same place.

Wilkins, Texas.

As Sam positioned his phone to take a picture of one of the postmarks, a text from Josh came in.

THEY'RE COMING BACK!

As he read it, he could hear the engine of a car pulling into the driveway.

26

4:10 p.m.

JIM PULLED his car into the driveway. Rhonda sat next to him and squeezed his hand as he killed the engine. They both looked in the back seat at Jack, who had fallen asleep on the drive home. Jim's heart broke for his son. Walking in to find your grandfather shot in the face and bleeding out was bad enough. He couldn't imagine having to witness it.

Fortunately, the trauma of it all had given Jack what the doctor called dissociative amnesia. He remembered seeing his grandfather standing in front of the work-table and then sitting in his mother's lap in the living room as the ambulance pulled up to the house. No recollection of anything in between. But the reality of what had happened soon became apparent to him and he became scared that he might lose his grandfather and close friend.

Jim understood that feeling. He had insisted that his father move in with him after his mother died. He said it was because he didn't want his dad to be alone, but after losing his mom, Jim couldn't stand the thought of losing his father, too. And over the past several months, they had grown closer than ever. But he never saw this coming.

Why did Dad do this? he kept asking himself. *I should have seen his depression. I could have helped him.*

Both the doctor and Rhonda had tried to tell Jim that it wasn't his fault and there was nothing he would have been able to do. That's, unfortunately, how depression works sometimes. But Jim wasn't buying it. His father didn't suffer from depression. It was something that detective had said. He had tried calling him to find out what they had been talking about. But so far, Sam Lawson hadn't called him back.

Jim lifted Jack out of the back seat and carried him inside as Rhonda walked beside him. He laid him down on his bed and turned to hug his wife.

"I need to clean the garage," he whispered.

"Do you have to do that now, Jack?" Rhonda whispered back.

He shook his head. "I need to be doing something."

Rhonda nodded and kissed him gently.

"He's going to be okay," she whispered, nodding at Jack.

But they both knew she was lying.

Still in a daze, Jim went to the laundry room and grabbed bleach, a scrub brush, and a bucket from the overhead cabinet.

Sam had scrambled into the shadows as soon as he heard the approaching car engine. Crouched low and unable to see what was happening, he tried to gauge where the Moore's were by the sound of car doors shutting and footsteps. He grabbed a handful of the postcards, then put the lid back on the box, carefully placing it on the bench. There was no time to put it back in its proper hiding place. He turned to make his escape but froze when he saw a figure heading toward the side door.

Jim walked absent-mindedly to the garage. Had he been paying better attention, he would have noticed that the police tape had been broken. Or he may have even noticed a man inside the garage scrambling to hide. He reached for his key as he grabbed the doorknob, only to find it was already unlocked. But he easily wrote that off to just forgetting to lock it earlier in the heat of the moment. He stepped into the garage and flipped on the light, surveying the horrific scene. Besides the pool of blood on the floor, there were blood splatters on the garage light, worktable, and garage door. His father's blood. Curiously, there was also a shovel and a fire poker splayed out on the garage floor.

Must have been the police, he thought.

Letting out a loud sigh, he got down on his hands and knees, pouring bleach on the bloody floor. He started scrubbing vigorously, the crimson stain turning pink but not going away.

Sam stood stiff as a board behind the stack of cardboard boxes, trying to figure a way out. He knew it could take hours to clean up blood stains. He didn't have that kind of time. But if Jim Moore discovered him, he'd have him arrested on the spot and he'd lose even more time. As his mind scrambled for a way out, he didn't even realize he was losing grip of the postcards he had been clutching. Until he felt one slip out of his fingers. He looked down helplessly as it seemed to float in slow motion to the ground. Maybe Jim wouldn't hear it over the sound of the scrubbing. Maybe he wouldn't notice it hitting the ground.

But in that moment, that split-second that seemed like an hour, Jim stopped scrubbing to survey his progress. In that moment, the postcard glided to the floor, making a *sssssss* sound as it slid out from behind the boxes. Both the subtle sound and the motion of the card sliding on the floor caught Jim's attention. He turned to see the postcard sliding to a halt on the floor.

He stared at it, trying to figure out both what it was and how it suddenly appeared. Then he let out a loud sigh.

That damn possum is back.

Not wanting to spook it, Jim quietly stood and crept backwards to grab a fishing net that was hanging on the wall. With net in hand, he took a slow, silent step toward the wall of boxes.

Sam held his breath, not sure what to do or where to go. He was cornered like a… well, like a possum.

Jim took another step. His next move would be to leap behind the boxes and slam the net down on his unwelcome garage rat.

As he readied his net, he was startled by a man's voice at his front door.

"Hello? Anyone home?"

Jim looked out the garage window to see that actor fellow standing on his front porch.

"What the hell?" he said, as he turned and stormed out of the garage.

27

4:20 p.m.

W~HILE~ J~OSH~ ~BORE~ the full force of Jim Moore's verbal wrath, Sam snuck out of the garage, scurried through the backyard, jumped a couple of fences and wound up on a street half a block away. Even though he couldn't fully hear what they were saying, it was clear Jim was yelling at Josh. Rhonda stood between the two men, trying to calm her husband down. Josh seemed to be apologizing profusely, but it didn't seem to be calming Jim down. He finally stormed back into the house, at which time Rhonda sent Josh back to his car. Josh sped away, barely slowing down enough for Sam to get in the truck.

"Oh, do you ever owe me," Josh said.

"Put it on my tab," Sam said. "What did you say to him?"

"I told him I just heard the news about his father and wanted to personally apologize."

"I can see he didn't accept it."

"He was pretty clear he wanted to beat the shit out of me," Josh replied. "He would have flat out killed you. Luckily, his wife was there to intervene. But he went inside to call the cops, so we need to get out of here quick."

Josh continued to drive Sam's truck, an honor of trust he didn't want to ruin by calling attention to it. But Sam was barely paying attention. He was too busy looking up the location of Wilkins, Texas, on his phone. When he found it, he let out a groan.

Wilkins was a tiny community in Central Texas, as far in the middle of nowhere as you could get.

"It's six hours away," Sam exclaimed.

"What's six hours away?" Josh asked.

Sam filled Josh in on the discovery of the postcards, the handwriting that matched Mullen, and the Wilkins postmark they all shared.

"That's got to be where he's at," Sam said. "But it's six hours away. I can't get there by eight."

"So, call Goldsmith. They've got to have agents closer."

"The closest is San Antonio. That's only two hours away, but... I've been thinking."

Josh waited for him to finish the sentence.

"Were you just bragging," Josh finally asked. "Or were you going to finish that sentence?"

Sam let out a sigh, as if he hated to share his thoughts out loud.

"Mullen has it in for me. That's why he took Carla. If anyone else shows up, he's just going to kill her. But if I show up, he may be willing to trade."

"That's insane," Josh protested. "You know that's insane, right?"

"You know I'm right."

Josh thought about it for a minute. As much as he hated to admit it, what Sam said made sense. But it didn't get them any closer to Wilkins. Then Josh had another idea.

"We need to go to my hotel."

"We don't have time for that," Sam argued.

Josh looked at Sam and nodded. "Trust me."

28

———

4:45 p.m.

SAM AND JOSH walked quickly down the hall of the hotel until they reached Room 307.

"You think he'll go for it?" Sam asked Josh as the actor knocked on the door.

"Can't hurt to ask," Josh replied.

After no one answered, Josh knocked again a little harder. This time, they heard stirring from inside.

"Do not disturb," a groggy voice yelled from inside.

"Guzman. It's me, Josh."

They heard more grumblings from inside the room until the door was finally opened by an overly tanned man in a white robe and a baby blue sleeping mask pulled up on his forehead. He looked at Josh and then at Sam.

"This can't be good," he muttered. He walked back into his room, waving the two familiar faces to follow him.

Alan Guzman was the producer of a Bigfoot movie that was being filmed in Quinton. Josh was one of the stars. He knew Sam because he had hired him to investigate the death of another actor in the movie.

"This is my Power Nap time and you know I'm not to be disturbed during Power Nap time," Guzman said. "Please don't tell me someone else has died."

"Sam needs a favor," Josh said.

"One that couldn't wait for an hour?" Guzman asked. "I thought this partnership broke up once you solved Decker's murder."

"You know about Ken Mullen, right?" Sam asked.

"The Replacement Killer. Who doesn't know?"

Sam proceeded to tell Guzman how Mullen had faked his death, then re-emerged to abduct Carla and how he believed Mullen was taking her to this small town in Central Texas.

"And you're telling me this because..." Guzman asked.

"He needs to borrow the plane," Josh interrupted.

Guzman was stunned by the request. He turned to Sam.

"You want to borrow the studio's private jet?" Guzman asked.

"It's the only way I can get to Carla before it's too late," Sam said.

"Guzman," Josh said. "You have to…"

Guzman raised a hand to silence Josh. You could almost hear the wheels turning in his head. Finally, he nodded.

"Okay. You got it. I'll make the call."

Josh and Sam both let out a sigh of relief.

Guzman reached for his wallet and pulled out a black credit card.

"As soon as you figure out where you can land the plane, let me know. I'll have my gal call ahead for a rental car. You'll need this. Just keep your receipts."

"I can't thank you enough," Sam said, visibly stunned it was that easy.

"You can work it off when you get back. I've got a few business partners that need looking into. Also, the story rights are mine."

"Sure. Whatever you want."

"Exclusive. Don't talk to anybody else. Movie. TV. Action figures. Lunch boxes. The whole shebang."

Sam nodded, not even truly sure what Guzman was talking about, but not really caring.

"Come on. Let's go," Josh said.

"Hold on there, Boy Wonder," Guzman said. "You're

not going anywhere. We have a movie to make, in case you've forgotten."

"But he needs my help."

"Do you not even check your phone? We're set to start shooting again tonight. We've got a lot of time to make up."

Josh started to protest, but Guzman cut him off.

"He gets the jet. I get you."

"It's okay," Sam said, eager to get going. "You've done enough."

Josh nodded. He had gotten so involved in his partnership with Sam, he'd almost forgotten about the movie.

Sam stuck out his hand, but Josh was having none of that. He grabbed Sam and pulled him into a hug.

"Good luck," he said. "If you need anything, call me."

Sam nodded, pulled himself away, and rushed out the door. He had a plane to catch.

29

5:00 p.m.

SAM WATCHED Tyler grow smaller out of the jet's window. He looked around at the plane's cabin. He'd never flown on a private jet and he had to admit, he was kind of disappointed. He was expecting something gaudy and opulent, like the Lisa Marie, Elvis's airplane at Graceland named after his daughter. Suede chairs, gold-plated seat belts, leather-covered tables and a private bedroom. But this jet just looked like a smaller version of a regular plane. Granted, the seats were larger and comfier and they were arranged differently, with some seats facing each other. And there were less of them. Only eight seats, to be exact. And he was the only person in any of them.

He wasn't alone, though. There was a pilot, a co-pilot and a flight attendant who introduced herself as Jo-Ann. Sam felt odd having them all being called into work just to transport him. Seemed like a tremendous waste of resources. But he certainly wasn't going to turn it down. This jet was the only possible way he could get to Wilkins before Mullen's deadline.

Jo-Ann brought him a fresh cup of coffee. He had asked if she could keep 'em coming the entire flight. This was really the first time he'd sat down and done nothing since this whole ordeal began and if he tried to catch a nap, he may never wake up.

Instead, he sank into his chair and ran through the events of the last 24 hours. It wasn't long before his mind wandered to thoughts about Carla. He refused to even entertain any thoughts of what Mullen could be doing to her, so he forced his focus to the wonderful moments they had shared.

He remembered the first day he saw her. He walked down to the morgue, holding his breath as usual but ready to talk to Bob Rodriguez. Instead, he was faced with an unfamiliar face. A very serious-looking woman wearing a white lab coat and her brown hair pulled back tight in a bun. She was intense, abrupt, and professional. He could tell she was smart and would put up with none of his usual bullshit. He fell for her right then and there.

It didn't take long for the ol' Sam Lawson charm to wear her down and they went out on their first date. He saw a different Carla then. Softer. Funny. A smile that melted his heart every time.

He closed his eyes as he remembered their first kiss. He had never felt lips so soft. Her hair smelled incredible. Her skin was... He shifted in his seat as his thoughts stirred up more than just memories.

Their relationship moved fast, but was not without its bumps. He was even rougher around the edges back then, and she pushed him away several times. But he knew she was the best thing that was ever going to happen to him and he needed to grow up. He wanted to become the kind of man that deserved the love of a woman of her caliber. That became the new goal. One that he fell short of almost daily. But, hey, at least he was trying.

Like with many of Sam's big life decisions, their engagement happened pretty spontaneously. They were already moving in together, but that was almost more practical. Her place was too small and his landlord decided not to renew his apartment lease. As they were bringing in boxes, Sam got caught up in the moment. He looked at this incredible woman – one he was well aware was way out of his league — and he dropped to his knees right in their new kitchen. He didn't have a ring, but she didn't care. She said yes, much to the delight of the four burly movers who were bringing in their furniture. One of them even started crying tears of joy.

He smiled at the memory. She was so happy, and he loved nothing more than making her happy. Still, he hemmed and hawed with the wedding date. Not so much avoiding it, but delaying it. When it came down to making it official that he would spend the rest of his life with this woman, he wasn't sure if he could do it. The rest of your life is a mighty long time. She was patient and took it all in stride. She knew how Sam worked and knew he wasn't going anywhere. He just needed time to wrap his head around what his heart already knew.

Sam's smile melted. He hated himself for ever even actually wondering if he could spend the rest of his life with Carla. Now that there was a chance he could lose her, he couldn't imagine a life without her.

He clenched his jaw. He was NOT going to let Mullen take her from him. He was going to find him. And he was going to get Carla back.

30

———

5:10 p.m.

CARLA WAITED until she felt sure Mullen was gone. She heard a door shut as the footsteps left the cabin, but no sounds of a car engine starting. He must be traveling on foot.

I won't be able to hear him return, she thought. *Do I even risk this?*

But she knew she had no choice. She was beginning to believe that Mullen was right about one thing. Sam wasn't going to find her. She had heard him talk about Mullen having various kill shacks all over Texas – probably many they still haven't found. And for all she knew, she wasn't even in Texas anymore. She was a tiny needle in a small haystack. If she was going to survive, it would be up to her.

She began to rock the chair side to side, building momentum to topple it over. As it finally began to fall, she braced for the impact. Her head banged against the floor, sending a bolt of pain through her skull. Her shoulder ached from taking the bulk of the fall and she prayed she hadn't dislocated it. But she didn't have time to assess her injuries. She needed to act quick.

She began to shimmy herself and the chair forward, slowly inching toward the knife on the floor. She had to not only move across the floor, but also turn so the back of the chair was closest to the knife. Then she would be able to grab it with her hands and hopefully cut herself free.

The chair banged and knocked as she moved and she thought about stopping to listen for any sounds signaling Mullen's return. But what would it matter at this point? It wasn't as if she could suddenly pull the chair back up and pretend nothing had happened. She was in it all the way. For better or worse.

Carla's ears rang and her vision was blurred. She felt sure she had a concussion. Her entire body was on edge, but she fought hard to keep her resilience. She shifted her position so her back was to the knife and began to push backwards.

Then she heard the unmistakable sound of footsteps approaching. Before she could even panic, the door opened and Mullen looked down at her.

"What the holy hell?" he exclaimed.

"I'm sorry," she bluffed. "I fell over. I called out for you to help me, but you weren't here."

"Jesus Pete," he murmured as he crouched to grab the chair and right it again.

He pulled it back to where it had been and examined the small bruise forming on her forehead.

"I told you not to move too much, didn't I?"

"I'm sorry," she replied, playing the victim and praying he wouldn't see the knife on the floor.

But he noticed her eyes glance toward it. Her heart sank as he turned and spotted the knife on the floor. He picked it up and sat it on the workbench next to the tools and other knives. His back was to Carla, but she could tell by the way he was breathing that he was angry. He turned around, shaking his head.

"I'm really, really disappointed in you, Carla," he said in a clipped tone. "I thought you were smarter than this. Now we're just going to have to do things differently."

He reached up on a shelf in the corner behind her and pulled down a blue nylon rope, shaking it in her face.

"I tried to be cordial," he said. "This is all on you."

He flung one end of the rope over an exposed

ceiling beam then pulled the end to a metal hook secured into the wall over the workbench. As Mullen tied the rope to the hook, Carla stared at the other end of it, dangling in front of her eyes.

"You could have left well enough alone," he continued. "What did you think you were going to do? Cut through your rope? Are you that stupid?"

"I panicked," she said. "I'm sorry."

Mullen shook his head, standing in front of Carla and bending forward to cut the rope binding her wrists. He quickly pulled her arms in front of her and Carla winced as sharp pain seared through her shoulders. Before she could even react, he had tied her wrists together again and then quickly tied that rope to the blue nylon rope dangling from the beam.

He then walked over to the hook and tightened the rope until it pulled Carla's arms over her head.

"Please," she muttered, knowing what was coming.

"You blew it, Carla," he said. "But you've left me no choice."

He walked back to Carla and cut the rope that was securing Carla's waist and ankles to the chair. He then yanked her up to a standing position and kicked the chair out of the way. They stood face to face and Carla saw the evil glee in Mullen's eyes as he pulled the rope until it pulled Carla off the ground.

Her body screamed in pain as he secured the rope

at the hook. He returned to stand in front of her. A twisted smile slid across his face. Having her suspended in front of him seemed to awaken another side of him.

"I know it hurts," he purred. "I'll give you something for the pain. But I want you to feel it for awhile. Consider it your punishment."

She leaned her head back in pain, focusing on the rope to help distract her. She followed it up to the ceiling beam it hung over. Then she noticed something.

The rope had shifted into a small slot in the beam and lay against a small piece of a metal brace. It gave her an idea.

She twisted her body to the side as if she was trying to free herself.

"I wouldn't do that," Mullen cautioned. "You're just gonna make yourself sick. I've learned that the more still you become, the less painful it is. Or it looks that way, anyway."

Carla looked down, as if giving up. She didn't want her eyes to betray her again. But as soon as Mullen turned away, she glanced back up at the rope above her.

It had moved slightly against the metal.

It was a long shot but, if she could keep the rope moving back and forth along the exposed metal, it might eventually cut through the rope and let her drop free.

31

6:45 p.m.

SAM EMERGED from the mid-size Gulfstream jet, which had landed in a local airfield twenty minutes north of Wilkins. A brilliant pink band of light along the horizon of rolling hills was all that was left of the day's sun. The flight was brief and Sam had spent it pumping himself full of coffee and playing out every worst-case situation he could possibly imagine. By the time the plane hit the ground, he was a frazzled bundle of nerves.

He had tried to call Goldsmith and Ramirez from the plane, but his calls didn't get through. Jo-Ann, the friendly flight attendant, had informed him there were problems with the jet's wi-fi. Sam was actually relieved. He knew he needed to call Goldsmith, but he was hesitant to pull them in too soon. For one, this could be another wild goose chase. But he also didn't need FBI agents showing up and agitating what he imagined would be a delicate situation. He knew Carla's best bet would be if he showed up alone. Even though Sam admittedly handled delicate situations like a bull in a china shop.

The private airport, which was comprised of a single runway and a small trailer home, was desolate. Sam imagined they didn't get many planes. A man emerged from the building and trotted toward him.

"You need help with anything?" he asked with a thick Texas accent.

"You know where I can rent a car around here?" Sam asked.

The man smirked.

"Gotta go back to San Antone for that," he said. "But if you're Sam Lawson, someone left a truck out front for you. Keys are in the cupholder."

Sam nodded, and the man walked past him to talk to the flight crew. Guzman had promised to have a rental car ready for him, but Sam was too cynical to believe he would actually come through. His silent gratitude for the act of kindness was enough to distract Sam from his worries for a moment.

Sam walked around the trailer to the parking lot, where he saw two cars. One was an old, dark green

GMC Sierra. The other was a shiny new, bright red Jeep Wrangler. Sam walked toward the truck, hoping it was the carriage awaiting him. But he knew better. The flashy Jeep was more in line with what Guzman would have picked out. Sam pulled the truck's door handle and sighed when he found it was locked.

Bright red Jeep it is.

Wilkins is a tiny community located right in the middle of the Texas Hill Country, a rural patch of Texas that spreads out just west of San Antonio and Austin. Considered the meeting place of the hot and humid American Southeast and the dry and arid Southwest, the region is fairly remote and home to more ranches than people.

Wilkins was one of several small towns in the area and was really not much more than a commerce center for neighboring ranches. A four-way intersection marked the hub of the town. Rows of modest buildings spread out in four directions from the center and included all the small-town essentials: a feed store, a gas station, a tiny diner and two churches (one Baptist, one Methodist).

Sam decided to start with the diner. Even though it was dinner time, there were only a few trucks in front. But in a town this size, everyone would know everyone.

He thought about his approach. People in this area were suspicious of federal agents, so it wouldn't serve him well to say he was helping the FBI. And people were also likely to protect one their own, even if that person happened to be a notorious serial killer. Sam decided to pretend he was an old cousin of Mullen's, coming into town to surprise him.

He checked his appearance in the rear-view mirror, the first time he had done so since this nightmare began. He looked like it, too. Disheveled with dark shadows under his bloodshot eyes and a rough five o'clock shadow across his tired face. He gave his cheeks a few slaps to wake himself up and ran his finger through his unruly brown hair.

His head buzzing from the coffee, he got out of the Jeep and headed into what would probably be his last shot to find Mullen and save Carla.

32

———

7:00 p.m.

A SMALL BELL attached to the top of the door announced Sam's entry. There were a handful of patrons, all now looking at the stranger that just walked into their diner. An elderly couple sat at a table in the center of the restaurant. A young family was attempting to keep their two toddlers occupied in a booth against the pale blue wall. And there were two men sitting at the counter in T-shirts and jeans. Each had a cowboy hat sitting next to his plate of food. A young but tired waitress stood across from them, and a cook peered through the open order window from the kitchen.

"Sit where you want," the waitress said matter-of-factly.

Sam decided to try his luck with the men at the counter. He nodded at them as he sat down, and they nodded back before returning to their food. The waitress handed him a laminated menu and put a glass of water in front of him.

"No special orders. If it ain't on the menu, we ain't got it."

"I actually was hoping you could help me, if you don't mind," he said in a thicker than usual Texas accent.

The waitress sighed.

"You another one of them reporters wants to get the common folk's opinions on the redistricting stuff? I can save you the time. We don't care."

Sam was thrown by the statement and took a second to re-gather his thoughts. He flashed a big grin and poured on the charm.

"I assure you I ain't no reporter. Hell, I don't even got no TV."

The waitress nodded, unimpressed and turned back to cleaning the counter area. Sam kept talking to the waitress but spoke loud enough for others to hear.

"I'm actually passing through. I'm from Grand Saline, headed to El Paso. But I got a cousin that lives around here and I wanted to surprise him."

He fake chuckled.

"We were joined at the hips when we was kids. You

ain't never seen two boys get in as much trouble as we did."

"What's his name?" the waitress asked without looking up.

"See. That's the thing. I ain't sure. I know that sounds crazy, but he used to go by Scooter Davis when we was kids. Then his mama re-married. Some big guy with one of those droopy mustaches. You know what I'm talking about? Comes down on both sides? Anyway, when she remarried they moved out this way and I ain't seen him since. His mama was my mama's big sister, and she got madder than a wet hen when they moved away. She wouldn't let us even say their name in the house. But I did overhear her once, when she was yelling at my daddy, that Scooter's stepdad adopted him."

By now he had captured everyone's attention and they were all looking at the animated, talkative out-of-towner, waiting for a point to the rambling story.

"So, I figure Scooter ain't Scooter DAVIS no more and I'm guessing, now that he's all growed up, he ain't likely to still be using Scooter."

"So, how do you think we're going to help you find a person without knowing his name?" the cowboy sitting closest to him asked.

Sam smiled at him. The cowboy was big and rough-looking and was probably familiar with the inside of a jail cell.

"I got a picture. Found it at my mama's house when she passed away, God rest her soul. I guess she made peace with her sister before she headed off to the Promised Land. Still kinda weird for her to carry around a picture of her nephew. Maybe she was stalking him. We'll never know. But I'm sure it's him. Even without a name on the picture, I recognized ol' Scooter right away."

Sam pulled out his phone, thumbing through until he came across the picture of himself with Ken. It was one Carla had taken when he had last visited. When Sam still thought Ken was an old friend just bored with retirement. Sam looked at the image. He pretended to still be searching for the picture but was actually quickly editing himself out of the one he had.

He held the picture up to the cowboy, who shrugged and shook his head. Sam walked around the diner and showed it to everyone.

"Any of you seen him? I figured he's working around here somewhere."

Everyone looked at the picture and shook their heads. An elderly woman pulled the phone close to get a closer look.

"Oh, I've never seen him before."

Sam let out a sigh. He had hoped he would catch a

break. Then he spotted a collection of photos tacked to the wall in the hallway to the restrooms.

"What are these?" he asked as he walked toward them.

"Just some pictures of townsfolk," the waitress explained. "Most of 'em are from last year's county rodeo."

She went on about the rodeo and how people came in from all over, but Sam wasn't listening. He was scouring through the photos, looking for anyone that might resemble Mullen. Sam reasoned that if no one recognized him, he probably wore a disguise when he was out in public, assuming he was ever out in public. It was a long shot, but it was all he had.

One photograph caught his eye. There was a man and woman in matching western shirts with face paint that, when they put their heads together, created the Texas flag. But Sam was more interested in the man standing behind them. He had a long grey beard and cowboy hat and was wearing sunglasses, but Sam would recognize that shit-eating grin anywhere.

Sam snatched it off the wall.

"Well, butter my butt! I think this is him!"

He frantically walked the picture around. "You know this man?"

The cowboy at the counter took the picture and gave it a long stare. He shook his head and passed it to the waitress. She looked carefully and then smiled in recognition.

"Oh, that's Earl Douglas," she said. "You mean to tell me Earl is your cousin?"

"Earl is Scooter!" he said. "You know where he lives?"

"Over at the Bader Ranch," the man beside him said.

Sam nodded, trying to force a regular breath. His entire body was buzzing.

"He's got a ranch?" Sam asked.

Everyone laughed.

"Earl? Hell no. He lives AT the Bader Ranch."

Sam waited for him to offer more, but that was all he seemed to be willing to share. Luckily, the waitress chimed in to fill in the gaps.

"He helps out Peggy. It's her place. But Peggy's getting up there and mainly gets around with a wheel-chair, so he takes care of things for her."

"Have you seen him lately?" Sam asked.

All the diner patrons looked at each other as they thought.

"I honestly can't think of the last time I saw him," the waitress offered. "He ain't come into town for a couple of months, at least. But that's normal."

"Can you give me an address?" Sam asked. "Tell me how to get there?"

The waitress winced.

"I don't know if that's information I should be giving out," she said. "For all I know, you're some crazy serial killer."

"Jesus, lady. First a reporter and now a serial killer. I better go check myself in the mirror. I must look really bad."

That got a laugh out of the cowboys. Then the waitress. It was just enough to disarm them a bit.

"Address won't do you no good," the big cowboy said. "You ain't gonna see a house number and GPS ain't worth a shit out here. But it's easy to get to. I'll draw you a map."

33

7:25 p.m.

AFTER DRIVING ELEVEN MILES, Sam was beginning to think he had missed the turnoff. It was growing increasingly dark and, with no streetlights, it certainly would've been easy to miss all but the biggest landmark. But just before Sam was willing to admit defeat and turn around, he spotted the Bader Ranch entrance. There was no gate. Just a limestone gravel road that turned off the main road with a large white arch running over it. The white enameled metal had caught the reflection of Sam's headlights and, as Sam slowed down, he noticed the decorative letter B hanging from the center of the arch. Nothing pretentious or showy. Just as the cowboy had described it.

Sam drove up the bumpy gravel path, which snaked its way through the rugged hills and yellow plains grasses until the Jeep's headlights shined on a modest two-story home. He cut the lights immediately.

Damnit!

He had meant to turn them off as soon as he turned on to the gravel road, but his adrenaline was pumping so hard, it had completely slipped his mind. If Mullen was in the house, he had probably already seen his Jeep approaching. Still, there was the chance he hadn't, and chance was all Sam had left.

He parked the Jeep a good hundred yards from the house and got out quietly, making sure to shut the door gently behind him. There were no yard lights or porch lights and, as far as Sam could tell, no lights on inside the house. Sam gripped his Glock pistol and crept cautiously toward the house. The terrain was rocky, and he struggled to walk quietly. Nothing seemed right about any of this. It was too dark. And too quiet.

When he got to the house, he walked cautiously up the gravel path and then slowly walked across the creaky wooden floor of the front porch, wincing with every step. Then he stopped at the door. What was he supposed to do now? Yell for Carla? Barge in? Knock?

It occurred to him that Mullen may not even be in the house. In which case, Sam was trespassing and could be the willing target of a trigger-happy Peggy Bader. He decided to knock. Politely.

The gentle knocks seemed to echo in the silence. He listened for any movement inside but there was nothing. He looked around for any signs of life. But there was nothing. No cars. No lights. Nothing.

When no one answered, Sam decided to walk around the house to check the back. He walked slowly and carefully, his fingers gripping his gun tightly. A blanket of stars spread across the night sky and, as his eyes adjusted, he found that the half moon was just bright enough to cast a pale glow over the area.

When he didn't find any cars parked behind the house, Sam felt more confident that no one was home. He walked up the rear steps and knocked on the back door. A bit louder this time.

"Hello? Anyone home?"

He jiggled the doorknob and was surprised to find it was unlocked.

"Hello?" he called out as he pushed the door open. "Mrs. Bader? The door was open. Is anyone here?"

He stepped into the pitch dark blackness of the room and called out again. When no one answered, he reached for the light switch with one hand, the other holding his gun in front of him. He flipped the switch quickly, fully ready for Mullen to be standing in front of him. The hallway light flashed on, and Sam was relieved that no one was waiting for him.

He walked through the house quietly, calling out Mrs. Bader's name but never getting a response. He looked for signs of life and saw a pile of mail on the dining table. Mainly bills and junk mail all addressed to Peggy Bader and all postmarked with yesterday's date. Sam spied a desk in a room opposite the dining room.

That must be her office, he thought as he crept over.

Sam knew a lot of these Central Texas ranches had small cabins for seasonal workers or hunters that would lease the property. If Mullen wasn't in the main house, maybe he was in one of them. Maybe he could find a property map or something in the office that could not only give him the lay of the land but also pinpoint other cabins on the property.

Sam looked around the room for anything that could help him. He rummaged through the papers on the desk and found nothing. There was another table underneath a large bulletin board. He shuffled through the papers scattered all over it, but found nothing. He started looking over the different notices and reminders tacked to the bulletin board and had almost given up hope when he realized there was something underneath the pinned notices. It looked like a map. He sat his gun down on the table and began furiously removing the pinned notices to get a better look. It was a survey map of the entire ranch.

The property was bigger than he thought. According to the map, it was just over 23,000 acres. Most of it was open range for cattle and sheep. But just as he had suspected, there were several smaller cabins scattered over the land. They were each marked with a different letter.

He could be anywhere, Sam thought.

Sam rummaged through the papers on the table again, looking for anything that could give him a clue. That's when he found an opened envelope addressed to Earl Douglas. Sam quickly pulled the contents out. He read the letter, trying to absorb its contents. He checked the postmark. Earl, or Ken, got the letter about four months ago. Right before he re-appeared in Sam's life.

His mind spun as he tried to process the information he had just read. But before he could even wrap his head completely around it, he got a strange sense that he was no longer alone.

34

———

7:30 p.m.

JOSH PACED BACK and forth across the fake cavern floor while a tall man in a Bigfoot costume sat on a boulder drinking Dr. Pepper through a straw. Members of the film crew worked around them, repositioning the lights for another shot.

"Jeez, man. You mind acting crazy over here," Chad McGinnis, the film's director, said from his canvas director's chair. "You're killing the vibe."

Without even acknowledging he heard his director, Josh walked off of the set and continued his pacing behind a wall of video monitors. It was killing him not knowing how Sam was doing.

Had he found Mullen?

What about Carla? Was she still alive?

Did Sam need his help?

He had tried calling Sam, but the call went straight to voicemail. Could be because of a lack of cell service in the Hill Country. Or Sam didn't want to be bothered. But maybe Sam was in trouble. He didn't want to keep calling. It could make matters worse. And he had left a message with both the local police and with the FBI office. But no one had called him back.

He had thought about just leaving the set and hopping in a car toward Wilkins. But he knew it was too long a drive. By the time he got there, it would probably be too late to help. Josh didn't know what to do. All he knew was he had to do something. Then a thought occurred to him.

"I've got to get something in my trailer," he yelled back to the director as he started running through the large warehouse that had been converted into a mini film production studio.

"Five minutes," Chad yelled back.

Josh flung the trailer door open and rushed inside, looking for the pair of jeans he had been wearing earlier. He found them balled up in a corner right where he had left them. He grabbed them and fumbled through the pockets until he found the business card he was looking for.

He frantically dialed the number on the card, rocking back and forth on the heels of his feet as he listened to the phone ringing. Finally, a woman answered.

"Nancy Hellard," she answered.

"Nancy! Hi! This is Josh Cole. We met earlier today?"

Nancy had been sitting in an upholstered chair in her modest hotel room, poring over notes she had gathered through various interviews. Her producer was breathing down her neck to come up with a story soon, but she was still holding back as she had promised. However, she was running out of patience. It was killing her she had the scoop on one of the biggest true crime stories in the nation and was just sitting on her hands.

There was something in Josh's voice, though. She leaned forward with interest.

"I know who you are, Josh. What is it? Everything okay?"

"I don't know," Josh replied. "But I need to find out. You still interested in that exclusive with a celebrity angle?"

"Do you have something for me?"

"Depends," Josh responded. "Do you have access to a plane?"

"How about a helicopter?"

35

7:35 p.m.

SAM TURNED to find himself once again staring into the barrel of a rifle. He sighed and slowly raised his hands.

"Who the hell are you?" the woman in the wheelchair demanded.

She was small, but was clearly not fragile. Her piercing blue eyes glared at him from behind a pair of bright red frame glasses and her thin lips seemed incapable of a smile. She held the .22 rifle to her shoulder, her finger on the trigger, and Sam had no doubt she would use it without hesitation.

He glanced over at his handgun that he had laid on the table earlier. She could easily get a shot out before he could grab it.

"Mrs. Bader. I'm so sorry. I didn't think anyone was here," he mustered.

"That don't give me any less reason to shoot you," she snapped back.

"I knocked, but no one answered. I called your name, I swear," Sam stammered. "Then I noticed the door was open, and I was worried something had happened to you."

Peggy Bader tightened the grip on the rifle.

"You still ain't answered my question, son," she said in a clip. "Who the hell are you?"

Sam quickly raced through a litany of answer possibilities, trying to decide which one would get her to lower the gun. He was a private detective looking for a serial killer? Sounds too far-fetched. He was an old friend of Earl Douglas? Then why the gun? Before he had gone through all possible scenarios, his mouth seemed to make the decision for him.

"I'm with Border Patrol," he heard himself saying. "And an old friend of Earl. Is he here?"

"Let me see a badge," Peggy demanded, the rifle still aimed at Sam.

With his left hand in the air still holding the letter he had been reading, he slowly moved his right hand to his back pocket and pulled out his private investigator badge. He held it up for her to see, still not quite sure what he'd do when she realized it wasn't a border patrol ID.

"Bring it here," she said. "Slowly."

Sam stepped toward her, his hand covering up the words PRIVATE INVESTIGATOR at the top of the picture ID. Hopefully, she would just focus on the shield and wouldn't bother reading it. Peggy leaned forward, squinting at the badge. She looked up at Sam suspiciously, then finally let out a loud sigh.

"Hell, I'm too blind to read it," she said. "But you didn't know that and only a fool would've showed a fake badge to a woman aiming a gun at him."

Sam relaxed a bit as she lowered the rifle. But he took notice that, even though the gun was now resting on her wheelchair's armrest, it was still pointed at him and her finger was still on the trigger.

"So, you here on official business or just to see Earl?" she asked.

"I came here looking for Earl," Sam said as he slowly put his ID away and lowered his hands. "But when no one answered, my Border Patrol radar went off and I came in to make sure everyone was alright. I'm sure you know about the drug traffickers moving through this area."

"Is that why you're going through my mail?" she asked.

"Just wanted to make sure I had the right house," Sam replied.

He raised the letter he had been reading.

"So, Earl does live here, right?"

"I don't know where he is."

Sam set the letter down on the table and kneeled so he was face to face with the old woman.

"Can you not tell me?" he whispered. "Is he listening? It's okay. You're safe now."

"What the hell is wrong with you?" Peggy asked. "I told you, he ain't here. So, he can't hear me. And I wouldn't care if he did."

Sam stood up.

"I need to find him as soon as possible. Do you have any idea where he is?"

"He's been gone a few months. I don't know when he's gonna get back."

Sam let out a deep sigh that sounded more like a groan.

This can't be a dead end, he thought to himself. *I'm running out of time.*

He looked up at the map.

"Could he be in one of those cabins?" Sam asked.

"Why would he be there?"

"Just humor me. If he was in town, could he be in one of those cabins?"

Peggy scowled at the question. She was also losing patience.

"I suppose he could be. But he ain't. He would have had to drive right by the house, and I didn't hear him or see him."

Sam studied the map. A dashed line cut behind one of the cabins and led back to the county road.

"What's this?"

Peggy squinted at the map.

"What's what?"

"This dashed line that runs between that cabin and the main road."

Peggy studied the map, then nodded.

"That's the old road," she said. "But it got washed out years ago when everything flooded. I don't think it's drivable."

"But you don't know for sure?" he asked, staring at the map.

This has to be it, Sam thought. *He could have fixed the road so he could get in and out undetected. Which means he's got Carla in that cabin.*

36

———

15 minutes earlier…

MULLEN HAD his back to Clara, whistling as he cheerfully cleaned the knives and tools on his work-bench. He turned, satisfied, and stared at her.

"I'm thirsty," he said. "You want some more water?"

Carla looked at him defiantly, still unwilling to give in at all. Mullen smiled and patted her cheek.

"Nah, you're fine," he said. "But I'll get me something."

This time, when he walked out of the room, he left the door open.

Carla took advantage of his disappearance to check her progress on the rope. She could see frays in it, but it was hard to tell how close it was to breaking. Using energy she had hidden from Mullen, she began to sway side to side. She felt something give. It was almost there.

"Would you look at the time?" Mullen said as he returned to the room. "It's almost eight. Guess who's not going to make it in time."

Carla had dropped her head again in feigned exhaustion, but her body was still swaying slightly. Mullen set his water bottle down on the desk and put both hands on her waist to steady her.

"You're gonna get seasick, darling."

Carla found herself now praying for the opposite of what she had been working toward. The rope needed to hold until he left the room again, or at least turned his back to her. She prayed that her body had enough energy to react quickly, but wasn't even sure if her legs would give out on her immediately.

As she considered her options, something caught her attention on Mullen's phone screen. He had propped the phone up and facing her so he could keep an eye on the surveillance feed. Carla could have sworn she saw a person walk by. Mullen noticed the way her eyes widened and turned to see what she was staring at.

"What is it?" he said. "Did you see something?"

He leaned forward to get a better look, but the person was gone. Mullen picked up his phone and toggled a dial in an app which controlled the camera. The view changed as he scanned the area.

"What did you see?"

Carla knew this was her moment. With all of her strength, she yanked downward, causing the rope to snap. She tumbled to the ground and fell forward, catching herself on the edge of the desk. Unable to stand, but fueled by pure adrenaline, she grabbed a hammer with her two bound hands as she fell to the ground, and swung it as hard as she could at Mullen's shins.

She felt the crack as the hammer made impact and Mullen yelled out in pain, falling to his hands and knees.

"You little–"

Before he could even finish his thought, Carla had raised to her knees and lifted the hammer over her head, dropping it down on the back of Mullen's head. Blood splattered and Mullen looked up at her, his eyes rolling back in his head before he toppled forward.

She didn't know if he was dead or just unconscious, and she didn't care. She needed to get out of the room, and the only way out was over his still body. Carla struggled to stand, using the desk as a crutch. She inched along the desk, past Mullen's body, toward the door. Her foot dragged along the floor and up against Mullen. Finally, dragging over his empty hand.

Mullen groaned and stirred, and Carla looked down in horror as he regained consciousness. She mustered all the strength she could to lift her leg over his hand, but it caused her to lose her balance and she collapsed forward through the doorway.

Mullen's groans grew louder, and he began to stir. Still unable to stand, Carla desperately pulled herself away from him, out of the room and into the small main room of the cabin. Directly in front of her, approximately ten yards away, was the front door.

She could feel her strength returning and she pulled herself up and crawled toward the door. Mullen's groans turned into horrific yells of rage and pain. Carla crawled faster to the front door. She reached up and gripped the doorknob, using it to pull herself up. As she got to her feet, she swung the door open. It was dark outside, and she had no idea where she was, but she knew she had no choice but to run. She looked back for the first time and saw Mullen. He was still laying on the floor where she had left him, trying to lift himself up. Knowing she couldn't waste another moment, she turned and stumbled into the darkness.

Mullen's head throbbed and pulsed. He could feel the blood trickling down his forehead. Seething with unbridled rage, he pulled himself up and lurched through the cabin and out the front door. Carla was nowhere to be seen, but Mullen knew she couldn't have gone far. Plus, he had the added advantage of knowing the area – even in the dark.

He limped his way to the side of the cabin and yanked a large black tarp off an electric ATV. Congratulating himself for keeping it charged up, he unhooked the charger cable and straddled the four-wheeler. It started up with a purr. One advantage of an electric ATV is they were much quieter than gas-powered models. That would make it easier for him to track down his escaped prey.

37

————

7:50 p.m.

SAM RUSHED through the tall grass, trying not to trip over all the loose rocks. He didn't want to drive to the cabin. Mullen would see him coming and there's no telling what he would do to Carla if that happened. He needed the element of surprise, which, unfortunately, also meant that Sam couldn't use his phone's flashlight to illuminate his path. The moonlight helped some, but the Hill Country terrain was rugged and Sam stumbled more than once.

He had given Goldsmith's card to Peggy and asked her to call and fill him in on Sam's whereabouts and the cabin he was headed to. He then advised her to stay inside and put away her rifle so incoming law enforcement didn't see her as a threat. Peggy had told him they SHOULD see her as a threat. She didn't like trespassers on her property, even if they were with the law. She was still yelling at Sam as he left the house, locking the doors behind him. Whether or not she really would call was out of his hands.

He checked the time. 7:50. He had ten minutes until the deadline. He had estimated the cabin was about half a mile from the main house. If he walked fast, he could get there in twenty minutes. Unfortunately, he didn't check the time when he left, so he wasn't sure how long he'd already been walking. It could have only been five minutes. Or it could have been fifteen. Sam picked up the pace, but immediately tripped over a large rock he hadn't seen.

He hit the ground with a thud and immediately heard the unmistakable rattle sound that could only mean one thing: a rattlesnake.

Sam lay perfectly still. He knew rattlers shook their tails as a warning. Because it could take weeks for them to replenish their venom, they would only strike as a last resort. Still, if they felt threatened in the least, they certainly wouldn't hesitate.

The rattling persisted and Sam figured the snake was probably coiled up about four or five feet in front of him. He had a few options. One, he lay perfectly still

until the snake wandered off. But there was no guarantee how long that would take or if the snake would
even go away. Sam didn't have that kind of time.
Another option would be to try to grab a rock to throw
at the rattler. But there's no telling which way the snake
would move if attacked. It could come right for him.
Plus, the sudden movement would surely agitate the
snake and it wouldn't hesitate to strike. The third option
would be to move backward very slowly, away from the
snake.

Sam had once watched a nature show about
rattlesnakes and thought he remembered they had
excellent night vision. Similar to a cat. Or was it a
nature show about cats having good vision? Either
way, he felt it safest to assume the snake could see
him in the dark. And he imagined that if he tried to
stand up, the snake could see him as a threat and
strike. He decided his best bet would be to crawl
backwards a bit. Maybe if the snake thought he was
retreating, it would back off. At the very least, he'd be
further away. Maybe the rattler wouldn't be able to
reach him if it decided to strike. If the snake didn't
perceive the movement as threatening, it may hang
back.

Sam spent a minute trying to calm himself down,
catch his breath, and plan his slow retreat. The snake's
rattle never let up, so Sam knew it was still on guard,

waiting for any sign of attack. Hopefully, it wouldn't read Sam's movement as one.

Sweat was pouring down Sam's forehead. It stung as it rolled into his eyes, and he squinted to try to wash them clean. His heartbeat thundered in his ears, and he took a deep breath.

Here goes nothing.

He began to very, very slowly inch his upper body back. The snake's rattle sped up and Sam froze. But the snake didn't strike. Moving as slowly and smoothly as humanly possible, Sam pulled himself up on all fours, still crouching low to the ground. Then he began to slowly crawl backwards. The loud rattle never let up, but the snake didn't strike out either.

So far, so good.

Sam crawled backwards until he felt he had put about five feet of distance between himself and the rattle. Then he slowly rolled back on his heels and stood, continuing to take more slow steps backwards.

Finally, the rattling stopped. Sam listened for any noise but heard nothing. He carefully reached down to grab a small rock and threw it in the snake's direction, hoping to scare it off. He decided to risk using his flashlight, turning it on to frantically look for his legless adversary. There was literally no sight nor sound of it. Satisfied it had slithered off, Sam shut off his flashlight and cut a wide berth around the area, prancing gingerly so his feet touched the ground as little as possible. Satisfied that he had skirted danger for the time being, he felt an adrenaline rush of relief flow over him. He continued on his trek, looking down to check the time.

Only two minutes left.

38

7:59 p.m.

SAM SPOTTED the faint silhouette of a cabin through the trees in front of him. A sliver of light peaked out from what must have been drawn curtains. He had found it. He checked the time. It was 7:59. With his gun drawn, he took off running and stumbling his way toward the cabin. He had no strategy. No plan of attack. With no time to waste, all he could do was hope the element of surprise would be enough.

He saw the door and ran toward it at full speed, turning his shoulder toward it and bracing for the impact. With a painful crash, he barreled into it, knocking it off its hinges. Sam toppled inside, falling to the floor and quickly rolling up on his knees, his gun raised in front of him.

His heart sank when he realized the main room of the cabin was empty. He stood as he studied the room. There was a single light bulb hanging from the center of it, casting a yellow glow and long shadows over the space. The door to a bathroom was to his immediate right. He could pretty much see all of it from where he was standing, and it was clear it was empty. There was one other room, the door slightly ajar and no lights from inside.

Sam held his gun in front of him, bracing for any unexpected movement, but trying to be cautious enough so that he didn't shoot Carla by mistake. He stepped toward the door, listening for any signs of life. But it was eerily quiet. As he walked, he noticed small blood spatters on the floor, but he tried to stay focused.

Sam reached the door, almost afraid to open it. What would he find on the other side? What if he was too late? What if Carla's lifeless body lay on the floor, much the way he had found one of Mullen's previous victims?

Or maybe she was still alive. Unconscious. Or even awake but bound and muzzled, so she couldn't make any noise. Her only hope being him. Right now.

He kicked the door open and stared into the darkness. The lone light bulb in the main cabin cast just enough light into the room for Sam to see it was empty. His heart sank.

He stepped inside and flipped the wall switch. Nothing. He spotted a Coleman lantern. That must have been the light source used for this room. He reached for it and noticed something else. The lantern was warm. It had been used. Very recently.

He lit the lantern and looked around, his stomach turning immediately. An assortment of knives, pliers and handsaws were scattered across the desk. There were jars of chemicals and rags. A stool was toppled to the floor, along with a hammer.

And there was blood.

There was fresh blood on the desk. On the floor. And on the hammer. Sam saw a piece of nylon rope. It was the kind Mullen had used in the past to restrain his victims. This room must have been where he kept her. Carla had been here. He knew it. But where was she now?

He checked the time. It was 8:02. Only two minutes! Why didn't Mullen wait?

Sam grew frantic and panicked. His mind raced. Two minutes ago, the cabin was within view and he would have seen if anyone had left. That meant Mullen didn't wait until 8:00. Maybe he had seen Sam coming and had taken Carla somewhere else. Maybe there was still a chance.

He ran out of the cabin. Partly to see if there were any clues where they could have gone, but also because he needed air. That's when he saw the truck parked along the far side of the cabin. He was so focused on the cabin when he ran in, he hadn't noticed it before. But why would the truck still be here if Mullen had left with her?

He checked the ground for tire tracks. One set of tracks clearly belonged to the truck. But there was another set. But what were they? They were too close together to be a car or truck. They had to be an ATV. But ATVs were loud. If he had just left in one, Sam would have heard it. Sam looked around where the tracks seemed to have started. He shone his flashlight along the wall and spotted something on the ground. It was a small black box with cables on either end. He picked it up to study it, and it all made sense.

Son of a bitch has an electric ATV.

Electric ATVs ran on battery power, not gas. Because of this, they were quiet. If they had just left, Sam probably wouldn't have heard it. But where would they have gone?

Sam went back inside the cabin, searching for any clues that could help him find Carla. As he looked, he noticed something strange. The blue nylon rope hanging from the rafters was frayed at one end. He spotted a smaller piece of matching rope about ten feet away.

That's odd, he thought. If Mullen cut her loose, the extra piece would have fallen straight down. Why was it way over there?

Then Sam had a thought. He stood where Carla had been dangling. He mimed breaking free from the rope and slamming his hands forward. That would have thrown the rope across the room. His eyes darted around the cabin again for more clues.

If she broke free, there would have been a struggle. Carla was strong, but no match for Mullen. She would have had to take him by surprise. Maybe hit him with something.

Like the hammer on the floor.

What if Carla had grabbed it? Sam's breath quickened as his theory seemed to be coming to life. He looked again at the stool on its side. That must have been where Mullen had been sitting. He acted out what Carla must have done, pretending to grab the hammer from the desk and swinging it at Mullen. He made a note of where he would have fallen. It would have given Carla a clear path to the door. As he retraced the imagined steps, he notices smaller, subtle blood streaks. As if a person had been dragged. Or they had dragged themselves away?

She must have taken off into the woods and once

Mullen pulled himself back up, he went after her on his ATV. But how long ago? And where were they now?

Sam walked back outside to where the ATV had been charging and scanned the darkness.

That's when he saw a flash of light deep in the woods.

39

8:05 p.m.

AGENT GOLDSMITH HUFFED AROUND the hanger at San Antonio International Airport, yelling at anyone that would listen.

"What do you mean, there are no other planes?"

"If you give me a few minutes, sir, I will try to find something," a flustered airport employee replied.

Goldsmith and his team had found another dead body in an abandoned warehouse in downtown Houston's east side. After securing the area, Goldsmith and team were returning to George Bush International Airport when he got the strange call from Peggy Bader.

Mrs. Bader had told Goldsmith that a 'suspicious fella named Sam Sawland or something told her to call'. It took a while for the FBI agent to decipher what Mrs. Bader meant, but once he did, he gathered his team on an FBI jet and headed toward the Bader Ranch in Wilkins. Unfortunately, it wasn't long after takeoff that the plane was forced to make an emergency landing in San Antonio due to some sort of equipment malfunction. The serial killer he had been tracking for years was only 140 miles away, but it might as well be 1,400.

Goldsmith had pulled out his phone to look for any other agents in the Wilkins area when he heard someone shouting his name. He turned to see a familiar face walking toward him. It was that actor who had been hanging around with Sam.

"Agent Goldsmith," Josh yelled as he ran across the tarmac to the FBI hangar. Security stepped toward him, but Goldsmith called them off.

"What the hell are you doing out here?" Goldsmith asked the actor.

"Man, am I glad to hear your voice," Josh replied. "I think Sam found Carla."

He started telling Goldsmith everything he knew, but Goldsmith stopped him.

"I already know," he said. "Unfortunately, I can't get out there. My plane is down for at least another hour and I can't find another one."

"I think I can help," Josh replied.

. . .

Goldsmith followed Josh across the tarmac but stopped cold when he saw the TCC helicopter. A pilot and two men were talking while the chopper was getting fueled up. Pacing near the back of the craft was a familiar-looking woman talking on her cell phone.

"You've gotta be shitting me," he mumbled.

40

8:10 p.m.

CARLA TOPPLED over a clump of rocks and fell to the ground. With her hands still bound, she couldn't break the fall, and she landed hard. But adrenaline and fear were pushing her now, and she scrambled back on her feet and fumbled forward into the darkness.

She had removed the duct tape from her mouth but didn't dare yell out for help. It would only let Mullen know where she was. She looked back to see if the headlamp was getting closer. When she first saw it, she had thought it was a large flashlight, but it moved too quickly. It had to be an ATV. Knowing Mullen was chasing her in a vehicle, Carla had veered off the trail and into the woods. He would be less likely to follow her into the thick woods. But she had no idea where she was running and could only hope it would lead to help. The trees were also clumped into small patches and kept emptying out into more open fields of low grass and brush. Whenever she hit an opening, she would duck low and race toward another group of trees.

She raised her arms in front of her to block the branches as they whipped and slashed at her. Every lash came with a sharp sting, but she crashed forward, praying she was running toward help. She thought about what she had seen in the surveillance video right before she escaped. She was certain it was a person, but who was it? And where were they? Her last sliver of hope wanted to believe it was Sam, and she ran forward, hoping she would somehow find him.

She looked back again. The headlight was gone. The ATV made very little noise, so it was hard to locate without the light.

Where did he go?

She reached the end of a thicket and stopped, looking at the open land in front of her. The moon cast just enough of a glow that she could make out another thicket of trees about twenty to thirty yards in front of her. But running to it would leave her exposed, and she had no idea if Mullen was nearby. Suddenly, a beam of light cut through the woods behind her. It was far enough away that she felt she could make it across the field before he got close.

She stumbled forward, forcing her legs to move as fast as they could. Still hobbling from the sedatives, her legs would occasionally buckle and Carla would fall again. But she would force herself up and keep staggering forward.

Over her labored breathing, she could hear the electric buzzing of the ATV as it moved closer. Worried she wouldn't make it to the woods in time, she summoned all her energy and pushed toward the trees. She had to get there before Mullen could get to the open field.

She was so focused on the treeline that she forgot to watch where she was stepping and slipped on another rock. Her ankle gave out from under her and she tripped and crashed to the ground. A burning pain seared through her ankle and up her leg. But she had to keep moving.

She gathered all her strength and pulled herself up again. She was only about ten feet away.

Then the sound of the ATV stopped.

Carla panicked and lunged forward to reach the edge of the woods. She lay flat on the ground, pulling her body forward and into the trees. She shimmied forward in an army crawl until she found a large tree and moved behind out, trying to steady her breathing. Then she listened.

There were enough rocks and branches on the ground that Mullen wouldn't be able to walk toward her without making noise. She tried to concentrate, trying to hear beyond her labored breathing and pounding heart.

Then the field behind her lit up. Mullen had turned on the headlight of the ATV. She heard the engine whirr as he started it up again, driving slowly through the field, searching. She stiffened back against the tree, praying she was hidden from view as she watched the beam of the headlight cut through the woods.

41

***

At the same time...

SAM RAN BLINDLY toward the moving light in the distance, tripping and stumbling over rocks and low brush along the way. The light had been moving slowly and in a haphazard pattern. Like it was looking for something. That only helped confirm his theory that Carla had escaped and Mullen was hunting her down. Sam ran even faster, gasping for air and wishing he were in better shape. But then the light stopped.

What did that mean?

A thousand thoughts ran through his mind. On one hand, he was relieved Carla was alive. On the other hand, he knew that if Mullen caught her, he'd dispense with any ceremony he had planned and kill her on the spot. He needed to find her first.

He wrestled with yelling out her name. Maybe hearing his voice would be enough to distract Mullen. Maybe it would turn Mullen's attention toward Sam, leaving Carla alone. But what if Sam was wrong? What if Mullen already had her? If Sam yelled, Mullen might do something drastic with his hostage. Sam decided he needed to better assess the situation before making his presence known.

He beelined toward the light, cutting through the woods. Small cedar branches whipped and lashed at him as he maneuvered through trees that only appeared as shadows in front of him. As he stumbled past one clump of trees, he slammed into thick brush. A chaotic frenzy of movement and crackling branches erupted out of nowhere. Sam fell backwards in total shock. The burst of havoc only lasted a few seconds, and Sam gasped for air as the sound of hooves dissolved back to silence. He must have spooked a family of deer.

Sam realized he was no longer holding his gun. During his deer debacle, it must have been thrown from his hands. He crawled on all fours, fumbling in the dark to try to find it. Then he noticed something was different. He stood up on his knees. It was dark. Completely dark.

Where was the headlight?

Sam looked all around him, confusion and dread welling up inside.

Then he spotted it. The ATV was facing away from him, so the light was harder to see. Plus, Sam had lost his bearings while looking for his gun and had been looking in the wrong direction.

He noticed the headlight still wasn't moving.

Had Mullen found her?

Or maybe he had her all along. Horrific thoughts ran through Sam's head as he barreled forward. Maybe Mullen was using the light to help him see as he buried her. Maybe he was too late.

"No. No. No. No."

Fury and panic overwhelmed him and, abandoning the search for his gun, he stumbled and clamored over the rough terrain toward the ATV. He estimated it was only about two hundred yards straight ahead. But the woods were getting thicker and harder to navigate.

Then he heard something. He stopped so he could hear better. It was a voice. It was Mullen's voice. Sam couldn't make out the words, but it sounded like he was calling out to someone. It had to be Carla. Which meant she was still alive.

42

8:15 p.m.

CARLA STIFFENED up against the tree, trying to stay hidden from Mullen. Then the ATV stopped. She heard the soft crunch of his footsteps as he got off of the ATV and stepped toward the woods.

"Carla," he sang in a childlike taunt. "Where are you?"

Carla held her breath, praying that her body wouldn't betray her hiding spot.

"That was not very nice of you," Mullen continued. "Catching me off guard like that."

She could hear him walking closer to the edge of the woods.

"That rope trick was smart. Dumb on my part. I

knew I should have used a chain," he said. "I just thought the rope would be more comfortable for you. I truly was thinking about what was best for you."

From the sound of his steps and the projection of his voice, Carla could tell he was still behind her, but walking in a different direction to her left. Without moving, she glanced in the opposite direction to see if there was a clear exit path. But it was too dark to see.

"Tell you what. I'll make you a deal," Mullen said. "You come out now and we'll just go back to the cabin. No harm, no foul. I'll get you something to drink. Make you something to eat. And I won't hang you back up from the beam. You can be comfortable in a chair.

"I mean, that has to be better than out here. Especially at night. There's rattlesnakes. Scorpions. Pretty sure there's been a couple of mountain lion sightings, too. But you're not gonna find any people. I can pretty much guarantee that."

Mullen seemed to turn and walk in Carla's direction. Her body tightened, but there was nothing she could do but stay perfectly still. Fortunately, it sounded as if he was still in the field and hadn't walked into the woods yet.

"I wasn't about to kill you," he said. "That deadline was just to torture Sam. We still have time. He just doesn't know it."

He chuckled out loud.

"I bet he's panicked right now," he said. "And he's going to torture himself knowing he wasn't good enough to save you."

Carla knew he was lying. Even in the best scenario, she was a loose end. And Mullen was too much of a professional to leave loose ends.

She heard a twig snap. He was walking into the woods. She pressed up against the tree, almost as if she was trying to dissolve into it. He couldn't have been more than five yards behind her.

"Come on, Carla. I'm tired. I know you have to be."

He stood behind her for what seemed like an eternity, so close she could hear him breathing. When he finally spoke, she almost jumped.

"Screw this," he mumbled.

She heard him turn and walk away. Then the ATV started up and drove away. Carla let out a sigh of relief as her body relaxed. But she didn't move. Not yet. She listened as the ATV stopped again, but now it was further away. He was clearly checking another section of the woods.

Carla kept waiting. Finally, satisfied that he had moved on, she pulled herself to her feet. She still wasn't sure where to go, but knew her brest bet would be in the opposite direction of where Mullen had gone. She would move slowly so he wouldn't hear her. It may take her all night, but she would eventually find a fence line or a house where she could get help. There was also the possibility she would run into whoever she had seen in that surveillance video.

She looked in the direction where she had last heard Mullen's ATV, then turned in the opposite direction.

Only to walk right into Mullen's arms.

43

———

8:20 p.m.

"You don't have to do this," Carla pleaded as Mullen yanked her back toward the ATV.

He held her arms behind her back and pushed her forward with a knife to her neck. She could feel the sting from the sharp blade as it pressed against her skin. She barely resisted. What was the point? She wouldn't be able to get away.

Her body seemed to collapse in on itself in surrender, taking with it any shred of fight. She was going to die and there was nothing she could do about it.

"I gave you every chance," Mullen said. "All you had to do was give up on your own. But now you've breached our trust yet again, and I am out of patience."

Carla's instinct was to argue with him. But she did nothing. She had lost any fight she still had in her. Tears welled up in her eyes as she gave in to her fate.

"We can't do it here," he said matter-of-factly. "You're not ready. I need to get you presentable first."

He leaned in close and sneered a whisper into her ear.

"I know just how I want him to find you."

Sam, she thought. *I'm never going to see Sam again.*

She started replaying, and second-guessing, every moment that led to this one. If only she hadn't been so quick to call off the police escort home. If only she had answered the phone when she got home. If only she hadn't tried to escape.

Mullen stopped her when they reached the ATV.

"Now how are we going to get you back?" he wondered out loud. "I suppose I could just drag you."

He laughed menacingly.

"Oh, come on," he snickered. "I was joking. Although..."

His taunts were cut short by a loud yell that seemed to come out of nowhere.

"Auuuggghhhh!"

Sam appeared out of the darkness, leaping at Mullen and sending both men tumbling to the ground. Carla toppled in the opposite direction.

He attacked Mullen furiously, but he was already

out of breath from running through the woods and Mullen was a much larger man. He pushed Sam off and struggled to his feet, spotting the knife that had been thrown from his hands. Sam, fueled by rage and adrenaline, scrambled to his feet and lunged at Mullen just as he reached the weapon. Mullen tumbled forward, accidentally swatting the knife away.

Carla watched the knife spin to the far side of the two fighting men and tried to figure out how she could get to it. Sam tore himself away from Mullen's grip and lunged at the knife, but he landed on the ground with a thud, just short of his target. The knife was still out of reach.

Mullen crawled over Sam to get to the knife, but Sam reached it first. Mullen grabbed Sam's hand, and the two wrestled for control of the weapon. Knowing he was no match for Mullen's strength, Sam bit Mullen's wrist. Hard.

Mullen yelled out in pain and released his grip on Sam's hand. Sam rolled over so he was straddling Mullen. He raised the knife to attack, but Mullen grabbed Sam's shirt and yanked him to the side. The force caused Sam to let go of the knife and it sailed through the air, nearly hitting Carla and bouncing off the headlight of the ATV.

Carla saw where the knife landed and ran toward it. At the same time, Mullen kicked Sam off of him, sending him flying backward. He didn't even realize he landed next to the knife and, as he frantically scrambled to get up, he accidentally swatted it away just as Carla was about to grab it.

"Sam!" she yelled.

"Sorry!"

He got up and rushed toward the knife. And Mullen. The two men punched, pulled and wrestled each other, both of them trying to grab the knife before the other.

They both stood, beat down and exhausted. Mustering all the strength he had left, Mullen landed a right cross that sent Sam spinning and then falling backward. His face hit the ground with a thud and he lay on his stomach. He pulled himself back up and stood, still ready for more. But when he turned, Mullen was holding Carla with the knife to her throat.

"I think you might want to think hard about your next move, old partner," Mullen sneered.

Exhausted and defeated, Sam raised his hands in surrender.

44

8:30 p.m.

SAM AND CARLA knelt side by side in front of the ATV, their hands duct taped behind them. They were both looking down to avoid staring directly into the blinding headlight of the ATV. Mullen stepped between the ATV and his hostages, creating an imposing silhouette.

"I have to say, I am beyond impressed," he said. "How the hell did you find me?"

He knelt in front of Sam.

"You got lucky, didn't you? I swear to God, you're the luckiest man alive."

Sam clenched his jaw but held himself back. Mullen grinned and gave Sam a little wink. He stood.

"Alright, you're unexpected arrival kind of changes my plans, but we can work with that."

"So, how long have you known you're gonna die?" Sam blurted.

Mullen froze, his back to Sam and Carla.

"I don't know what you're talking about."

"I saw the letter. Back at Peggy's place. I can't pronounce the name but I know it's some deadly cancer and you're Stage 4, which means you probably don't have long to live. Is that why you're doing all of this? Your grand farewell?"

Mullen flinched, but only for a second. He turned and walked over to Carla, grabbing her by the shoulders and repositioning her so she was facing Sam.

"I want you to be staring into her eyes," Mullen growled as he walked over to Sam and repositioned him so he was facing Carla. "I want you to watch her die. I'm going to slit her throat right in front of you. You're going to stare into her eyes as she begs for you to help her and you won't be able to do a damn thing about it."

He knelt in front of Sam, pointing the knife in his face.

"I want you to know that you're not good enough. You don't deserve her. Or anything. You're a joke."

Sam laughed and shook his head.

"Is that what all this is about? You're jealous of me?"

"I'm not jealous. I'm fed up."

"No. I get it. I was always the cute one. Plus, I'm guessing you have some serious abandonment issues. Your partners kept leaving you. Me. Kaster. Even your old partner in crime, Cutter."

Sam looked directly into Mullen's eyes to make sure the words hit. Mullen kept a poker face but paused for just a second. Just enough for Sam to know he hit a nerve.

"This was always supposed to be a two-man operation, wasn't it? But Cutter was all talk. He bailed on you. And then completely turned his back on you. You kept trying to pull him back in, but he just ignored you. He hated what you were doing. Do you know he tried to kill himself?"

"He never tried to kill himself," Mullen snapped back.

Sam shrugged.

"He's lying in a coma right now. Bullet to the face. How do you miss your own face? Nothing personal, but you were probably better off without him. Doesn't seem like he's good at the whole killing thing."

"Shut up!" Mullen yelled. "You don't know anything!"

"I know everything," Sam lied. "He confessed it all to me."

Carla stared at Sam, shocked by this revelation. She looked up at Mullen and could tell he was growing more and more agitated. Sam was up to something.

Mullen stood. Sam had clearly hit the nerve he wanted and he could tell Mullen was unraveling. He'd keep bluffing. Buying time. When Mullen wasn't watching, he had grabbed a sharp rock and was using it to slowly saw through the duct tape that was binding his hands behind his back.

"This whole 'clean up the world' crusade was his idea, wasn't it?" Sam continued. "I bet it started back in Beaumont. Both of you in it 50/50. But you were hungrier. Beaumont was small potatoes. You knew there was more work to be done, so you convinced him to transfer to Houston with you."

"From what Cutter told me, he was the mastermind behind it all," Sam lied, trying to keep Mullen distracted.

"He was never the mastermind," Mullen yelled back.

Sam ignored him.

"You enjoyed the killing, didn't you? It scared the crap out of Cutter. So he bowed out. Moved back to Beaumont to get away from you."

"I didn't need him," Mullen snapped. "He couldn't do what needed to be done."

He stepped toward Sam, gripping the knife hard.

"But I'm not afraid to do it," he snarled.

"You know he kept all the postcards you sent him?" Sam asked.

It stopped Mullen in his tracks.

"Kept them all in a little metal box. It was kinda cute. But that's probably not why you sent them, was it? They weren't mementos. You were taunting him. You weren't going to let him walk away from it all. Sending those cards was your way of keeping him involved. I'm guessing it's why he tried to kill himself. So good job there, old friend."

Mullen shook his head, but said nothing. Sam could tell all of this information was throwing him off.

"Is that your grand plan? You're gonna die, so you're taking all your old partners with you? A wee bit over-dramatic, don't you think?"

Mullen's face grew hard, and his lip curled into a sneer.

"I'm done talking," he said, as he stepped toward Carla.

Sam sneered back.

"Yeah. Me, too."

His arms now free, Sam lunged at Mullen, and the two men fell to the ground. Mullen raised the knife at Sam, but Sam pushed his hand back. The knife cut into a tire of the ATV and it hissed as the air escaped. Then Sam lifted Mullen up by the collar and punched him hard in the face. Mullen's head snapped back and hit the hard engine of the ATV. As he fell forward, Carla stood up. And when Mullen got on all fours to try to stand again, Carla kicked him hard in the stomach. Mullen collapsed to the ground and rolled on his side in pain. Filled with rage, Carla kicked him hard right between the legs. Mullen let out a loud moan and doubled over in pain. But Carla wasn't done. She kicked him again. And again. And again. Mullen looked up at her in shock and fear.

"Stop," he whimpered.

Carla answered with a ferocious yell as she kicked him hard in the face, knocking him out cold.

She reared her foot back to kick him again, but Sam pulled her away, turning her toward him and holding her close.

"It's over," he whispered, trying to calm her down. "It's over."

Carla's rage slowly dissolved into relief. The tenseness drained from her body and she collapsed into Sam's arms, sobbing.

Sam cupped her face in her hands and kissed her hard.

"I thought I had lost you," he said, holding back his own tears as he kissed her again and again. "I thought..."

"You're not going to get rid of me that easily," she replied.

She stepped back and motioned behind her back. "You think you can free me now?"

Sam had forgotten her hands were still bound behind her back. He spotted the knife near Mullen's feet and grabbed it, quickly slicing the duct tape from her wrists. She quickly spun around and threw her arms around Sam.

"I love you, Sam Lawson," she said before kissing him tenderly. "But we need to tie this bastard up before he comes to."

45

8:45 p.m.

SAM AND CARLA sat on the ground exhausted, leaning back on the ATV. The headlight was still on, shining a spotlight on Mullen, who lay on the ground in front of them, face down and still unconscious. His hands were bound behind him with duct tape, and his ankles were taped together as well.

"I guess one of us needs to walk back to see if we can get help," Sam said.

"You have shoes," Carla replied.

"You'll be okay out here alone with him?"

"You should be more worried about him."

Sam looked at Carla's bruised face. He examined the cuts on her arms and legs.

"My God, Babe. What did he do to you?"

"I did this to myself. Running through that brush," she said. "Is it bad?"

"You're beautiful," Sam replied, caressing her swollen cheek. "But we need to get you to a hospital."

"I'm fine," she replied, leaning her head into his hand.

Sam kissed her on the forehead and struggled to his feet. She attempted to pull herself up, and Sam reached down to help her.

"I don't want to leave you," he said.

"You're afraid to walk through the woods alone, aren't you?"

"I mean, I heard there were mountain lions."

She smiled, then cocked her head.

"You hear that?" she asked.

"Oh, Jesus. You heard one, didn't you? I told you. There are legit mountain lions out here."

She put her hand over his mouth to quiet him. Then he heard it, too. It was a helicopter. And it was getting closer. They both looked up as a helicopter headed toward them, a giant searchlight cutting through the night sky. They raised their hands to block their faces from the bright light and strong downwash of air.

"Way to go, Peggy," Sam said out loud, assuming the

ranch owner had called Goldsmith and given him the location.

But he became confused when he saw the blue TCC logo on the side of the helicopter.

How the hell did the media get here before the police?

As the helicopter hovered above them, shining the searchlight down on the scene, a couple of sheriff's deputies cars emerged from the woods and raced toward them.

Sam's confusion only grew when the helicopter landed and Agent Goldsmith emerged, his gun drawn and pointed in their direction.

"You okay?" he yelled to Sam and Carla.

"You steal a helicopter?" Sam yelled back.

As sheriff's deputies jumped out of their cars, Goldsmith rushed over to Sam and Carla, noticing Mullen laying on the ground.

"I see you got my message," Sam said.

"I did," Goldsmith said, kneeling to handcuff Mullen. "But all you gave me was the ranch. It's a big ranch."

"How did you find us out here?" Carla asked.

Goldsmith grinned.

"Your golden boy here swallowed a tracking device yesterday. Once we knew the general area, I was able to pick it up and it led us right to you."

He winked at Sam. "I'm gonna need that back from you when you're done with it. Don't flush it."

All the commotion stirred Mullen out of his unconscious state and Goldsmith yanked him to his feet. Mullen was confused at first but slowly realized what was going on.

"I'm so glad you woke up," Sam said. "I didn't want you to miss out on this moment."

He looked at Carla and grinned malevolently.

"Thanks for a good time," he said.

"Rot in hell," Carla spat.

Mullen locked eyes with Sam.

"You're lucky," Mullen sneered.

Sam stepped forward and patted Mullen on the cheek.

"You think I don't know that?" Sam said quietly with a smile. "It's a burden I bear every day. You, on the other hand? There's no punishment hellish enough for what you deserve. I hope that cancer eats at you slowly and painfully until you beg for death."

He stepped back to let the agents take Mullen away.

"Jesus, that was a little over the top," Carla said.

"Too much?" Sam asked. "It was too much, wasn't it?"

Carla grabbed Sam and kissed him. He pulled her closer, and they continued to kiss, forgetting anyone else was even there.

Josh, Nancy Hellard, and the film crew climbed out of the helicopter. Nancy immediately readied her mic and directed her crew toward Sam and Carla. But Josh, noticing the private moment Sam and Carla were enjoying, pulled their attention in another direction — away from Sam and Carla to the police cars where Goldsmith was taking Mullen.

"Looks like you're gonna get more than one exclusive."

They ran toward Mullen to try to get a quote and Josh looked back at the couple, still lost in each other's embrace.

46

One day later

CARLA SPENT the rest of the night at the Metropolitan Hospital in San Antonio. Sam never left her side. In addition to all the superficial cuts from running through the woods at night, she also had a mild concussion and a twisted ankle. But, compared to the injuries that Mullen's other victims sustained before he killed them, she was lucky. Still, the biggest scars would be psychological and were bound to haunt her for years to come.

When Carla wasn't being poked and prodded by the doctors, she was being cross-examined by Agent Goldsmith. Finally, Sam intervened, asking Goldsmith to let her rest and promising he could follow up when they returned home.

Before he left, Goldsmith pulled Sam aside.

"Just got word that Cutter Moore has pulled out of his coma," he said. "Thought you'd want to know."

"You know what's going to happen to him?"

"That's up to the Smith County D.A.," Goldsmith answered.

He took a deep breath and his tone grew more somber.

I'm sorry I doubted you, Sam," he said. "I should have trusted your instincts."

"No apology necessary," Sam replied. "I'm not a very trustworthy guy."

After twelve hours of observation, Carla was finally released. She sent Sam to the store to get her some new clothes, including a long-sleeved shirt to cover the cuts on her arms.

Guzman, who was happy to pamper his new cash cow, had sent his jet back to San Antonio to bring the couple home. They now leaned back in their seats as Jo-Ann, the flight attendant, poured them both a glass of champagne. They clinked their glasses and took a sip. Sam, not much of a champagne fan, tried to hide his lack of enthusiasm. Carla, on the other hand, savored the taste.

"I still can't believe this is how we're going home," she said.

"I told you. We've got friends in high places now," Sam replied.

He motioned to Jo-Ann.

"I really appreciate this. I do," he said. "But do you have anything stronger back there?"

Jo-Ann smiled.

"We have anything you want, Mr. Lawson."

"How about some really good whiskey?" Sam asked with a devilish grin.

Jo-Ann smiled and walked back to the galley to retrieve a top-shelf bourbon. Sam looked at Carla and shrugged.

"What's the point of having a private jet if you can't have your drink of choice?"

Carla smiled and snuggled in close to Sam.

"I really thought I had lost you," he said. "I honestly don't know what I'd do if that ever happened."

"You're not going to lose me, Sam," Carla replied, kissing him on the cheek. "If a serial killer with a vendetta can't tear us apart, nothing can."

"Oh, yeah," Sam said. "I almost forgot."

He reached into his jeans pocket and retrieved the

engagement ring she had thrown off her hand when Mullen abducted her.

"I think you dropped something," he said with a smile.

She turned to him, putting out her hand, and Sam slipped the ring on her finger just as Jo-Ann returned with his whiskey.

"Oh, my God!" Jo-Ann exclaimed. "Did you just propose?"

They both looked at the excited flight attendant and decided not to ruin her moment.

"Now I just need to get him to follow through on it," Carla said, showing the ring to her.

They both stole a smile as Jo-Ann looked at the ring.

"This is so exciting," she said. "Oh, my God. I'm sorry. I'll give you some privacy."

She scurried off to the cockpit and Sam and Carla could hear her squealing in delight as she shared the news with the pilot and co-pilot.

"About this," Sam said to Carla. "I've been thinking."

"Sorry. No take backs."

"I don't want to wait," Sam replied.

Carla smiled and kissed him.

"I don't either."

Sam shook his head.

"No. I don't want to wait. At all. We can still have a

party and reception and all that stuff later. But let's do it now."

Carla seemed confused, not understanding what Sam was saying.

"Okay," she said cautiously.

"Great!" Sam beamed and kissed Carla. "I love you so much."

He leapt out of his seat and approached the cockpit. Carla watched as the pilot smiled and nodded. Jo-Ann jumped up and down excitedly, clapping her hands.

Sam returned to his seat, a huge grin on his face.

"What is going on?" Carla asked.

"You said you were okay with right now, right?"

"What are you getting at?"

"We're going to make a slight detour," Sam said. "I hope you don't mind."

Carla looked at him in disbelief, then looked up at Jo-Ann, who was beaming at her and clapping her hands.

"What have you done, Sam Lawson?"

"We're going to Vegas. Let's get married. Now. Let's just do it."

Carla laughed at what she thought was a joke, but the earnest look on Sam's face quickly convinced her he was serious. She absentmindedly reached up to her bruised forehead.

"Sam. I don't know."

"First off, you're beautiful. Second, we don't have to take any pictures. We'll do a proper wedding later. All I know is I love you and I don't want to wait any longer. You go through life thinking you have all the time in the world but this whole mess made me realize that nothing is guaranteed. And if I die tomorrow, I want to die as Carla Davenport's husband."

Carla grinned.

"I'm trying to decide if that's romantic or morbid."

"There's just one small catch," Sam said.

He looked at the front of the plane where Jo-Ann was still beaming.

"I had to promise her she could be your maid of honor," Sam said. "She's so excited."

Carla laughed.

"Well, we don't want to let her down, do we?"

She kissed Sam gently then looked deeply in his eyes.

"Let's go to Vegas," she said, a huge smile spreading across her face.

THANK YOU FOR READING BEFORE HER LAST BREATH

If you enjoyed this book, be sure to leave a review wherever you bought your copy. A review can go a long way in helping other readers find this book.

ENJOY THESE OTHER SAM LAWSON MYSTERIES

COMBUSTIBLE - Sam Lawson Mystery 1

BENEATH THE SURFACE - Sam Lawson Mystery 2

DARK HARBOR - Sam Lawson Mystery 3

DEADLY REPUTATION - Sam Lawson Mystery 4

DEATH ON LOCATION - SAM LAWSON Mystery 5

Also by David K. Wilson:
RED DIRT BLUES

LEARN MORE AT davidkwilsonauthor.com

GET A FREE COPY OF *BOUND BY MURDER*
This fun and riveting mystery novella e-book goes back
to the first murder case when Sam Lawson and Ken
Mullen were partners.
It's available for free at **davidkwilsonauthor.com**

ACKNOWLEDGMENTS

Thank you to so many, including those listed here:

• Regina Riddle and Rena Grubbs for your beyond-appreciated support, encouragement, suggestions and friendship. Thanks for putting up with all of my late night questions as I muddled through this.

• My band of beta readers, including Barbara Fournier, Lorraine Evanoff, Shelly Upchurch, Yvonne Pelletier and James Hewiston. You have no idea how much I value your opinions and advice.

• Nicole McCutcheon, who keeps my website looking more professional and put together than I am. And who also saved me in a pinch by designing the cover to this novel (and knocking it out of the park).

• My colleagues in the book community, for encouraging and inspiring me.

• My friends and family. I truly couldn't do any of this without you.

Finally, thank you to my loyal readers, Facebook and Instagram followers, and newsletter subscribers for going on this journey with me. I hope I keep you entertained along the way and look forward to many more adventures!

ABOUT THE AUTHOR

David K. Wilson grew up in East Texas, surrounded by enough colorful characters to fill the pages of hundreds of books. In addition to being the author of the popular Sam Lawson Mystery series, David is also a seasoned ghostwriter and screenwriter. He currently lives in upstate New York.

Sign up to receive news and information about David's next novel at davidkwilsonauthor.com.

facebook.com/davidkwilsonauthor

goodreads.com/davidkwilson

instagram.com/davidkwilsonauthor

www.ingramcontent.com/pod-product-compliance
Lightning Source LLC
Chambersburg PA
CBHW030819210726
48290CB00002B/666